3 2222 0044 9287 4

WITHDRAWN

MONDAY'S CHILD

MONDAY'S CHILD

Brenda Beamon-Isabell

Praise for *Monday's Child*

"Monday's Child is the story of a mother's desperate fight against the system. Brenda Beamon-Isabell has poured out her heart in writing about the horrible deeds done to a disabled child and the cover-up that went on after it was discovered. If you love stories that show what courage and infinite love can do, this one is for you."

MARILYN MEREDITH, AUTHOR OF THE TEMPE CRABTREE SERIES, DEADLY OMEN, UNEQUALLY YOKED, GOLDEN EAGLE PRESS, AND EPPIE AWARD NOMINEE FOR KACHIMA SPIRIT, WWW.HARDSHELL.COM

"This book has taught me to never look over the little people."

KAREN HICKS

"Children are the most innocent human beings. The number of abused children that I saw in my profession as a Trauma Technician was overwhelming. This novel is heartbreaking, compelling, gripping and emotional. Brenda Beamon-Isabell's novel was written with feeling and empathy. A must read."

PEARLIE CASTON, TRAUMA TECHNICIAN AND DAY CARE PROVIDER

"Monday's Child is a mother's devastation after entrusting her physically and mentally handicapped son to the Melbourne Public School System. Beverly Monday's emotional betrayal and cover-up by the teacher, as well as the School System, is truly every parents' nightmare. Hats off to Brenda Beamon-Isabell for coming forth with such a dynamic story."

DENICE A. LEVERINGSTON, MILWAUKEE PUBLIC SCHOOL EMPLOYEE

" Brenda Beamon-Isabell chronicles the trial of a teacher, principal and school system sued for the abuse of a cognitively disabled little boy, Bryce Monday. <u>Monday's Child</u> . . . a literary masterpiece . . . presents the human side of many difficult issues . . . parenting and education of a disabled child, race relations and drunk driving. The courtroom drama . . . riveting . . . the constant windows into the emotions and experiences of Bryce's family . . . Beamon-Isabell has created a work of fiction about a mother whose intense emotions . . . her love for her . . . disabled child, along with the pain and devastation she experienced when he was abused. Gaining insight into the pain that abuse causes and the corruption that is possible in schools makes <u>Monday's Child</u> well worth reading."

YOUTH TODAY NEWSPAPER, WASHINGTON, D.C.

"We are pleased to inform you that we are happy to obtain a copy of your book." <u>MONDAY'S CHILD</u>. *"It will be included in our National Resource and Information Center. Your publication will be a welcome addition, and will surely enhance the resources available to our constituents."*
U.S. DEPARTMENT OF LABOR
OFFICE OF THE SECRETARY – WOMEN'S BUREAU
WASHINGTON, DC

"Monday's Child is about the discovery and cover-up of the physical and verbal abuse experienced by Bryce Monday. . .
from the public school system that was suppose to take care of him. Bryce's mother embarks on a difficult journey through the discovery of the abuse to the ensuing trial and the stress that takes its toll . . . It is a story of affirmation and self-discovery with the awareness that our children must never be overlooked or taken for granted."
NATIONAL COALITION AGAINST DOMESTIC VIOLENCE
DENVER, CO

"*MONDAY'S CHILD* first novel by Brenda Beamon-Isabell . . . uncovers the startling truth that school officials knowingly hired a teacher who did not have the qualifications mandated by the state . . . to teach handicapped children."
THE CHALLENGER NEWSPAPER
WILMINGTON, NC

"MONDAY'S CHILD by Wisconsin native Brenda Beamon-Isabell
. . . through the testimony of other teachers, Bryce Monday, an eight year old boy with a mental capacity of a nine-month old baby was physically abused by his teacher."
THE MILWAUKEE TIMES

Copyright © 2000 by Brenda Beamon-Isabell.
Front Cover by Artist Ed Miller A/K/A Akinshiju

Library of Congress Number:		00-190395
ISBN #:	Hardcover	0-7388-1629-9
	Softcover	0-7388-1630-2

All rights reserved. No part of this book may be reproduced or transmitted in any form or by any means, electronic or mechanical, including photocopying, recording, or by any information storage and retrieval system, without permission in writing from the copyright owner.

This is a work of fiction. Names, characters, places and incidents either are the product of the author's imagination or are used fictitiously, and any resemblance to any actual persons, living or dead, events, or locales is entirely coincidental.

To order additional copies of this book, contact:
Xlibris Corporation
1-888-7-XLIBRIS
www.Xlibris.com
Orders@Xlibris.com

CONTENTS

PREFACE 13
ACKNOWLEDGEMENTS 15
CHAPTER ONE 17
CHAPTER TWO 23
CHAPTER THREE 25
CHAPTER FOUR 28
CHAPTER FIVE 36
CHAPTER SIX 44
CHAPTER SEVEN 55
CHAPTER EIGHT 63
CHAPTER NINE 70
CHAPTER TEN 73
CHAPTER ELEVEN 77
CHAPTER TWELVE 80
CHAPTER THIRTEEN 82
CHAPTER FOURTEEN 85
CHAPTER FIFTEEN 92
CHAPTER SIXTEEN 99
CHAPTER SEVENTEEN 102
CHAPTER EIGHTEEN 107
CHAPTER NINETEEN 111
CHAPTER TWENTY 116
CHAPTER TWENTY-ONE 135
CHAPTER TWENTY-TWO 141
CHAPTER TWENTY-THREE 152
CHAPTER TWENTY-FOUR 156
CHAPTER TWENTY-FIVE 164
CHAPTER TWENTY-SIX 172

CHAPTER TWENTY-SEVEN	180
CHAPTER TWENTY-EIGHT	184
CHAPTER TWENTY-NINE	195
CHAPTER THIRTY	198
CHAPTER THIRTY-ONE	206
CHAPTER THIRTY-TWO	209
CHAPTER THIRTY-THREE	213
CHAPTER THIRTY-FOUR	216
CHAPTER THIRTY-FIVE	218
CHAPTER THIRTY-SIX	222
CHAPTER THIRTY-SEVEN	225

*This book is dedicated
to the person who inspired me to write it,
my son, Victor Paul Dunlap, II.
I love you with all my heart.*

Mom

Suffer the little children to come unto me,
and forbid them not:
for of such is the kingdom of God.

St. Mark 10:14

PREFACE

For the silent cries of developmentally disabled children, for those who have suffered at the hands of an abuser, may God protect you and always keep you safe.

I pray that our Lord and Savior grant us the strength and courage to be your voice and to speak out, even cry, for help on your behalf.

Brenda Beamon-Isabell
January 21, 2000

ACKNOWLEDGEMENTS

Everything that I am I owe to God. It is through him, by the grace of his glory, that my blessings flow.

Where do I begin? Only my name appears on the cover, but many people contributed to making my dream come true.

To my writing instructor and noted author, Marilyn Meredith, you helped me every step of the way. I finally understand character POV.

To my five readers: Stella Hill—The first person to read, edit and critique Monday's Child. I'll always be grateful for your editing skills, input and support. My dear friend, Juanita Davis—I am eternally grateful to you for the front cover idea and for making time to read my manuscript; but more importantly, thank you for being such a wonderful friend. Janice Williams—Thank you for agreeing to be a reader. Your friendship, support and constructive criticism is uplifting. Grace Uhlenkamp—You took time from your travels/retirement to be a reader. Thanks for your friendship and for always being in my corner. Karen Hicks—You made me feel important when you put aside James Patterson's novel to read mine. Thank you for your input.

Many special thanks to my readers for their time, honesty and support. I am forever indebted to all of you. I hope you're ready for the next one.

Warm thanks to my friends, Elaine Tartt and Cheryl Holmes. Although you live far away, your support and encouragement has always been close.

Maybe it was something as simple as "Hang in there", "How's it going", or "Don't give up" that was expressed to me during this lengthy process. I would like to thank those people for their continued support and encouraging words: J.T. Brown, Andrew Caston, Carrie Isabell, Deloris Hughes, Teresa Roebuck, Ellen Weber, Julius Horton, Jr., Rivest Dunlap, Sherill Gill, Karen Shilling, JoAnn Haack, Regenia Sellers and Bonnie Edwards.

To my beautiful daughter, BreAnne Dunlap, thank you for the voice activated recorder. Writing while driving is hard to do, especially when you're a two-handed driver. I love you.

To my entire family, to numerous to mention by name, thanks for your continued support and love over the years.

To the entire staff at Xlibris Corporation, much appreciation for making my dream of being published a reality.

Last and most certainly not least, to my husband, Charles Isabell—Your love, patience and support has always been a constant in my life. Those countless hours at the computer deprived us of time together. All the meals you prepared allowed me more time to write. I love you and am grateful for having you in my life. Mr. Isabell, you now have my undivided attention. I'm all yours.

CHAPTER ONE

Ella Walker watched Bryce Monday as he refused to drink his milk from the cup. Jennifer Reinhart's face transformed into a hideous mask of anger. Ella knew the teacher didn't like being told "no" by anyone—and especially a retarded child like Bryce.

It had become a constant battle between Jennifer and the tiny boy, and Ella feared for him.

Ella winced as she watched Jennifer squeeze Bryce's cheeks in a vicious attempt to make him open his mouth. Bryce tried to wiggle out of her grasp and squealed in pain.

Bryce was eight-years-old. At birth, he was diagnosed as having an unusually small brain, and because of this, was developmentally disabled. He was small for his age, and weighed twenty-five pounds and was only three-feet tall. He was pigeon-toed and had a rigid, jerking motion when he walked. Locks of naturally curly black hair smothered his oval-shaped head. His skin tone was smooth like peanut butter and his teeth as white as piano keys. His smile could brighten any room.

Jennifer Reinhart was the teacher in the developmentally disabled classroom at Carter Elementary School in the Melbourne Public School System in Melbourne, Wisconsin. She had been a teacher for eight years.

Jennifer shrieked, "You're going to drink this cup of milk."

Bryce tried desperately to free himself, but wasn't strong enough. He cried and screamed the only two words he knew—"Mommy, No."

He tried to bite Jennifer's hand, to free himself from her clutches, but he was no match for her.

She released him and Bryce tried to run.

His behavior angered her more. Bryce hobbled to the other side of the room.

Ella stood at the wooden rectangle table on the other side of the room where the other four children in the class were seated and stared, traumatized by Jennifer's behavior. Ella was the Handicapped Children's Assistant in Bryce's Classroom. Her duties were to assist the teacher.

Bryce limped to the table.

Ella waited by the table with the other children, speechless, watching Jennifer.

Trembling, Bryce dropped to his knees and crawled under the table. Jennifer scrambled after him, squatted down, grabbed him by both ankles and dragged him, face down, to the middle of the floor. She put one knee in his back and placed both of her hands behind his head, forcing his face to the floor. His lips smashed, Bryce groaned in agony. He squirmed in an attempt to free himself, but she was too strong.

It was eight-fifteen and the children always had cereal for breakfast. Ella placed bowls in front of the children, poured corn flakes and milk, but continued to glare at Jennifer. She wanted to stop her but didn't know what to do.

Rebecca was eight-years-old and autistic. She twiddled her fingers and moved her head in circular motions. Jonathan, eight and Maggie, seven, both with Down's syndrome, rocked back and forth. Aaron, a six-year-old, normal at birth who suffered brain trauma when struck by a truck and dragged for two blocks, sat in a state of oblivion. The children's disabilities were so severe they had little idea of what was happening to their classmate.

Ella looked at the phone mounted on the wall at the entrance. She glanced at Safety Joe, the life-size doll of a policeman at the door. If she went to the phone and threatened to call the police; maybe, Jennifer would leave Bryce alone. The bright yellow walls plastered with multi-colored alphabets and numbers gave a false illusion of happiness and contentment. Ella wanted to jerk Jennifer away from Bryce but knew, if she did, she could lose her job.

Bryce relaxed. Jennifer started to release him, but Bryce resisted again. Angrier, Jennifer reapplied force to Bryce in an effort to control him.

Bryce struggled to free himself but his twenty-five pounds were no match.

Jennifer was five-feet seven inches tall and weighed one-hundred-eighty pounds. Her loose clothing made her look ten pounds heavier, and older than her thirty-five years. Jennifer had reddish, straight shoulder-length hair and a face full of freckles. Her stern, pinched expression reminded Ella of a mean Army Sergeant.

Bryce finally surrendered, and no longer moved. Ella continued to stand at the table next to the children, totally stunned.

Ella usually spoke her mind. If she didn't like something, she spoke up. She was not one for beating around the bush. But she acted totally out of character as she remained on the other side of the classroom and, though furious, didn't interfere as Jennifer physically abused the tiny black boy.

Unable to keep still any longer, Ella said, "Oh my God, you're going to kill him. For God's sake, let him go."

Still holding Bryce down on the floor, Jennifer glared at Ella. "Need I remind you I'm the teacher and you're the aide?" Jennifer yanked Bryce to his feet by his arm. He staggered as she pulled him over to the table by his ear and plopped him down on the chair. He began to sob.

Jennifer stamped her foot and clapped her hands. "Stop that crying. I'll not have that either."

She grabbed the carton of milk and a cup from the table and poured Bryce another cupful of milk. "All you have to do is take this cup and drink the damn milk. If you can eat it on the cereal, you can drink it from a cup."

Jennifer grabbed Bryce's hands and forced him to hold the cup. Shaking, he continued to whimper, tears pouring.

Jennifer turned to Ella. "Pour the other retards a cup of milk while I clean up this mess." She went to the closet and grabbed the mop.

Ella shook her head in disgust as she poured milk for the other children.

Jennifer panted as she mopped swiftly. "You know, Ella, you'll have to stop being so emotional with these kids. You can't let them walk all over you."

"His mother told you that he don't like milk in a cup. Why can't you just pour it over his cereal like you said you would?" Ella asked.

Bryce hated drinking milk from a cup. He did, however, love cereal. Bryce's mother told Jennifer on the first day of school. At that time, Jennifer didn't seem to have a problem with the suggestion, but now Jennifer was determined to change him at whatever cost.

"You know he can't even feed himself. He makes a total mess and I'm sick and tired of cleaning up after him. His mother treats him like a baby. That's his biggest problem."

"Why don't you tell his mother if you feel that way."

Jennifer stopped mopping and stared at Ella. "Look, I'm not paid to raise these kids. I'm only paid to teach them. He's my problem for only three more months. While he's in my classroom, he'll do as I say. He'll either do it willingly or by force."

Ella was stunned by Jennifer's words. "Listen to yourself," she said. "Bryce screamed in pain. You hurt him." She sat down. Ella fed Maggie a spoonful of cereal. Aaron started to pound on the table and Ella gave him a drink of milk.

"He was not in pain. He thinks if he screams, I'll let him go and he'll have his way. It works with you," Jennifer patted her chest, "but not with me."

"I would never grab him, or any child, the way you did. These children are disabled. You know better than to call them retards." Ella stood.

Jennifer stopped mopping and gaped at Ella. "You'll do whatever I tell you. I'm the instructor in this classroom and you're merely the helper. I'm the one with the education, not you. Your application for this position indicated many years in the school system, but not much experience with children. Your insignificant certificate is of no comparison to my degree."

Ella had worked in the Melbourne Public School System for twenty years. She'd held such positions as custodian, crossing guard and worked in the cafeteria serving food and washing dishes.

Ella always worked part-time until about a year ago when her husband of twenty-nine years died suddenly from an aneurysm. Her only child, a twenty-seven year old son named Larry, was living in Michigan, so she decided to work full time to keep busy. Since she always loved working around children, she decided to work with kids who had special needs. This was an area in which there was a great need for teachers and aides.

She took a night class at City College and became certified as a Handicapped Children's Assistant. She was hired full-time six months ago.

"It doesn't take a degree to know when a child is being mistreated." Ella warned. "You may be the teacher in this classroom, but I'll not have someone half my age disrespect me. Bryce is afraid of you. I've never had a child who was afraid of me."

Fifty-four-years old, Ella was five-feet tall, weighed one hundred forty-eight pounds. Her gray hair was a perfect match for her bronze colored skin. Ella was everybody's grandmother and all the kids loved her. A mother and grandmother, she knew all about raising children.

Jennifer rolled her eyes. "Like I said, Ella, I'm in charge and you'll do as I say, or else."

Ella stared at her, hands on hips. "Or else what?"

Suddenly, Bryce threw his cup of milk across the room. Jennifer dropped the mop and ran toward Bryce. Grabbing his arm, she yanked him out of the chair onto the floor and dragged him to the middle of the room. She positioned him face down and pulled both of his arms behind his back. She placed her knee over his hands to hold them in place.

Ella gasped.

Jennifer rested her other knee on Bryce's butt. She forced his face to the floor. Bryce screamed out in pain. He started to cry and cough uncontrollably. He stopped resisting and became silent.

"He's not breathing." Ella rushed toward Jennifer and Bryce. "Lord, Jesus, he's not breathing."

Jennifer released Bryce, and pulled him to his feet. He was limp as she stood behind him, her arms around his waist to hold him up.

Ella started to pray out loud. "God, please let him be okay."

Bryce's head hung forward. Jennifer swayed him from side-to-side and softly sang *Ring Around The Rosies*. Perspiration dripped down the side of her face.

After a few moments, Bryce coughed.

"Thank you, Lord," Ella said.

Jennifer continued to sway and sing. Bryce stopped coughing after a few seconds and smiled. The color returned to his face and he breathed normally.

CHAPTER TWO

Ella jumped up from a deep sleep. Sweat soaked her gown. She couldn't get Bryce's screaming out of her head. She climbed out of bed around midnight and paced all night. She couldn't get the image of Jennifer's abusive behavior out of her mind. She wanted to physically restrain her, but her job was her livelihood and she couldn't afford to lose it. At the same time she knew Bryce could be seriously hurt—or killed.

Ella was in constant torment. She had to protect Bryce. The endless abuse to this child and not knowing what to do about it was overwhelming. Maybe she could let Bryce's mother know and make her promise not to reveal her source. Or the police?

Ella's two-bedroom home felt claustrophobic. She had to do something. If it were her son, she'd want to know. Tears stung her eyes. How much longer could Bryce endure?

Ella opened the beige drapes in the living room. All was calm and still outside. The world was asleep and the burden of her guilt weighed heavily on her mind.

She flung her body on the black leather recliner, buried her head and prayed out loud. "God please help me to do what is right. Give me the strength and courage to keep Bryce safe."

Ella settled into the chair and stared up at the brass ceiling fan. She saw Bryce's face on each of the blades. He moaned in torture. She closed her eyes tight, but Bryce's anguish had not been erased when she opened her eyes. Ella leaped to her feet, turned off the lights and paced in the dark.

She went to the kitchen and opened the refrigerator. She reached for the carton of milk and Jennifer's horrid face appeared on the carton yelling, "Drink the damn milk from the cup you, retard."

Ella slammed the door. She rushed to the sink and splashed her face with cold water. Leaning over, with her face buried in her hands, she wept.

Ella returned to the living room and sat on the leather sofa. Moments later she sat on the love seat, then found her way back to the recliner. What was she to do? She knew she'd be just as guilty as Jennifer if she allowed this repulsive treatment of this child to continue. She argued with herself all night.

CHAPTER THREE

Friday was a half-day of school for the students because there was a teachers' meeting in the afternoon. Ella was happy Bryce would only have a few hours with Jennifer.

It was seven-ten and Ella prepared the table for the children who would be arriving in twenty minutes. She went to the steel cabinet at the back of the classroom and got five bowls and spoons from the shelf and placed them on the table. She returned to the refrigerator next to the cabinet and grabbed the box of cornflakes from on top and placed it on the table.

Ella watched Jennifer from the corner of her eye as she went back to the cabinet and retrieved cups for the children. She positioned a cup next to four of the five bowls.

Jennifer ripped the page from the calendar on her desk to Friday. She erased the word "Thursday" from the chalkboard behind her desk and wrote "Friday" in capital letters. She went to the cabinet and acquired five fold-up chairs and placed them horizontally in front of her desk. Jennifer always started the day by having the children sit in front. She would call them one at a time, to help them become familiar with their name.

Jennifer asked, "Why only four cups and five bowls? Is one of the children not coming? I didn't get a call from anyone."

"No." Ella commenced to pour corn flakes into the bowls.

Jennifer walked over to Ella. "Then why?"

Ella exhaled slowly. "I'll feed Bryce today. No sense in trying to force him to drink from a cup. It's a half-day of school and let's try to make it through the morning without any conflicts."

Jennifer scowled. "And you'll clean up his mess too."

Ella rolled her eyes.

It was about seven-forty-five when Jennifer and Ella went downstairs to greet the children. The bus arrived moments later.

When the door of the bus opened, Ella quickly stepped in front of Jennifer and got on the bus. Jennifer followed. Ella went directly to Bryce's seat and unhooked his harness first. He rocked back and forth with a smile on his face. She led him by the hand to Maggie's seat and unhooked her. She then helped the two children off the bus and up the stairs to the classroom. Jennifer arrived shortly after with Rebecca, Jonathan and Aaron.

"Ella, next time I'll let you know which students to remove from the bus."

Ella didn't respond. She didn't want to say anything that might possibly make Jennifer angry. Ella knew Bryce would become the target of the teacher's rage.

After Jennifer and Ella removed the children's coats and book bags, they helped seat the children in the chairs in front of Jennifer's desk. Bryce smiled at Ella as she led him to the last chair on the right. Maggie was next to him. Ella stood behind Bryce and caressed his hair and his smile grew.

Jennifer seated Rebecca next to Maggie, then Aaron, with Jonathan on the left. She stood in front of Jonathan and repeated his name. "Your name is Jonathan." She pointed. "Jonathan is your name." Jonathan clapped briskly and rocked back and forth. She moved in front of Aaron. "Aaron is your name. Your name is Aaron." Aaron never responded.

Rebecca's high-pitched uncontrollable laugh echoed throughout the room as Jennifer repeated her name.

Maggie tilted her head back and opened her mouth. Her tongue traced her lips as she mumbled undefined utterances. Jennifer smiled and didn't bother to repeat her name.

Jennifer stood in front of Bryce and Ella saw her smile subside. "Bryce is your name."

Bryce looked up at Jennifer and slobber trickled from the side of his mouth. Jennifer grabbed a tissue from the box on her desk and started to scrub Bryce's mouth. "For God's sake look at you. You're foaming at the mouth like a rabid dog."

Bryce began to kick and shake his head rapidly from left to right. He kicked Jennifer in the shin and she grabbed him by both ears. "Stop it. Stop it this instance."

Bryce bellowed in distress. Tears surged from his eyes.

Ella walked in front of Jennifer, breaking her hold on Bryce's ears. Ella lifted Bryce from the chair, put his head on her shoulder and gently patted him on the back. She carried him to the other side of the room and sat at the breakfast table, Bryce cradled in her arms. "I'll wipe his mouth."

Jennifer squinted at Bryce and then at Ella. "Don't you ever undermine me in front of these retards again."

Weeks went by and Ella never revealed to anyone what was going on in the classroom, but always intervened whenever Bryce became prey to Jennifer's vicious and brutal attacks.

CHAPTER FOUR

Jennifer was home sick with stomach flu and wouldn't be in until the next day. Thank God for small favors. At least Bryce would be safe the first day back after Spring break. Ella knew something had to be done about the situation. She couldn't stand what was happening.

She could go to the principal and, maybe, he would have compassion for the little defenseless boy and stop the wicked bitch from hurting him again. Ella knew she'd be taking a chance, since the principal had a reputation for catering to the white employees at Carter.

Maybe, she ought to leave it alone. After all Bryce was going to a different school in September, so he wouldn't have to suffer at the hands of Jennifer again.

Melbourne Public School System rezoned their district to include an addition to Putnam School. The school bordered Melbourne's district and the addition put the school just outside. Rezoning to include the school caused reassignment of children who lived in the area where Bryce resided.

June was two months away and Ella knew something had to be done before Jennifer returned to school on Tuesday.

Ella thought about telling Bryce's mother the next time she came for a visit, but she couldn't do that either. She had to go through the chain of command, which meant going to the principal. It was not her place or position to tell Bryce's mother.

Ella finally decided that she would go to the principal after school.

* * *

It was track and field day at Drey Park and the entire school would attend. The park was located two blocks from school and all the children walked to the park. It was like a huge parade.

This was an annual event and the students participated, competing against each other for prizes in running and jumping. Even though Carter's disabled children could not participate, it was nice to be able to take the children out. The weather was a comfortable seventy-two degrees.

Fran Harrison had been assigned to help Ella with the children in Jennifer's absence. Fran had officially retired a year ago but agreed to substitute whenever she was needed.

The two women went through the day with no conflict or difficulty with each other. Fran had substituted several times at Carter and was familiar with the children in the exceptional education classroom.

Everything flowed smoothly. Ella was amazed at how well they interacted, not because they were both African Americans, but because they were close in age and had similar goals.

Fran was good with the children. She always greeted each one with a hug. When Maggie finally learned how to hold a spoon without assistance, Fran rewarded her with a kiss on the forehead. She always showed tenderness and concern for the students.

Ella and Fran sat at the picnic table with their children and watched the events of the day. The boys and girls went through their usual routines, rocking back-and-forth, continuous circular head motions, blank stares and drooling.

Maggie and Jonathan sat on one side of the table with Fran in the middle. Ella sat on the other side of the picnic table between Bryce and Aaron and Rebecca sat next to Bryce.

The children loved being outside. Bryce seemed to especially love the feel of the breeze. Every time one came pass, he would hold his head back, smile, and fall back into a daze.

The activities ended at two-thirty. The children returned to school around three o'clock. Once the children boarded the bus, Ella and Fran returned to the classroom.

Fran asked Ella, "Is there anything else to do before I leave?"

"No, that's it. I wanted to make sure the lights were off. You know, Fran, I really enjoyed working with you today. The children had such a good time."

"Thanks, I loved being here."

"It would be nice if they kept you instead of Jennifer Reinhart," Ella said.

"I know what you mean. I had the pleasure of working with her about a month ago when you were out ill. She doesn't understand these children at all. But Jennifer's young and she's still learning. I'm fifty-nine years old. I've been around for a while. All in all, she's okay. She might be a little rough around the edges, but, like I said, she's young."

"I didn't realize you filled in for aides. I thought you were contacted if a teacher didn't come to work."

"I do it all. I report wherever I'm needed. It doesn't matter if it's for a teacher or an aide."

At first Ella wondered if, maybe, Fran had seen Jennifer's tactics with Bryce since she had worked with her before, but decided she hadn't. Ella didn't want to be straightforward and ask, but she had to know. Maybe, Fran could help Ella understand what was going on before she talked to the principal.

"When you filled in for me, Fran, did you ever see any of the children upset or crying?"

"I do remember I was late the day I had to sub for you. As I walked in the classroom, the door was slightly cracked. I looked in and saw Bryce crying. I asked Jennifer what happened and she said he bumped his head against the wall."

Ella figured the bitch probably pushed him and he hit his head. "What did Jennifer do?" she asked.

"Well, she hugged Bryce and started to sing *Ring Around the Rosies.*"

* * *

Robert Clayborn has been principal at Carter for ten years. During this time he developed a reputation for being an "Uncle Tom," a sell out, and an embarrassment to his race because he married a white woman. He was known for showing favoritism to the white teachers over the blacks. In fact, a couple of the black teachers had filed grievances against him with the teacher's union for unfair treatment.

Forty-one, Mr. Clayborn was a man of great stature. His two-hundred fifty pounds was distributed evenly. His hairline receded to the middle of his head, leaving only traces of his black hair. His midnight skin was smooth and absent of shaving bumps. The black frame bifocals that rested on his nose was a perfect match to his skin. Mr. Clayborn was married to Susan, his wife of twenty-two years. They lived with their sixteen-year-old son, Eric, in Lake Hills, a predominantly white neighborhood.

Susan worked full time as a real estate agent and Eric attended Lake Hills High School in Lake Hills School District.

Mr. Clayborn sat in his office and worked on the school newsletter. He hadn't expected anyone after school, so was surprised when Ella knocked on the open door of his office.

"Mrs. Walker, this is a surprise. Come in." Mr. Clayborn stopped writing, removed his glasses and put them on the desk.

Ella entered, closing the door behind her. "Mr. Clayborn, I apologize for not making an appointment."

"No problem, have a seat." He pointed to the chair opposite his desk.

"There's been something going on in our classroom I think you should know about."

Concerned, he asked, "What is it, Mrs. Walker? You seem so upset."

"I am."

"What's the problem?"

"I don't like the way Jennifer Reinhart handles the children, particularly Bryce Monday."

"I'm not sure I understand. What do you mean? Handle?"

"She uses undue force on Bryce. I've seen her squeeze his arms and shake him."

"Mrs. Walker, Ms. Reinhart is always pleasant and talkative. I visited her classroom on conference day and the children's parents found it hard to depart. She definitely has the gift of gab. She's always friendly and shows such fondness for all children with special needs. What was the boy doing?"

"Mr. Clayborn, I don't think what Bryce was doing has anything to do with it. Regardless of her reason, it was enough force to cause him to yell in pain."

Ella stared at Mr. Clayborn, both of her hands flat on his gray steel desk. "She calls the children retards. I've also seen her push Bryce to the floor, press his face to the floor with her knee in his back. Bryce screamed because he was in pain. He stopped breathing."

Mr. Clayborn stood. "You know, Mrs. Walker, I saw the same thing you just described."

Ella sighed with relief and sat down. "You see what I mean. You've got to do something, Mr. Clayborn. I think you should call Bryce's mother. We need to have a meeting, as soon as possible, so we can tell Bryce's mother what's been happening to her son."

"I questioned Ms. Reinhart when I heard the child scream. She assured me he was only screaming to make her release him and that Bryce, in no way, was in pain."

"After what I've told you, you can't possibly still believe that lying white witch. You have to do something before she hurts this child."

"Wait, Mrs. Walker. Let's not jump to conclusions. We're dealing with a delicate situation. Please don't expect me to react differently because the child is black and the teacher is white."

"Jennifer will be back tomorrow." Ella pleaded. "Call his mother and have a meeting. Please, Mr. Clayborn."

"I need to speak with Jennifer first. Let me hear her side of this story. I must be fair."

Ella wondered if Bryce was white and Jennifer black, if he'd react differently.

"Okay, Mr. Clayborn. Will you do it tomorrow?"

"Yes. And if I think there's a problem, I will definitely contact his mother and inform her. But, Mrs. Walker, I will be the one to call Bryce's mother, not you."

"I know the procedure. That's why I came to you first."

Mr. Clayborn walked around the desk and shook Ella's hand. Ella started towards the door.

"Mrs. Walker, I'll be in touch. I have a meeting tomorrow, but I will speak with Ms. Reinhart as soon as I can and get back to you."

Ella left.

The last thing Mr. Clayborn wanted was friction from another black employee. It was bad enough he had reverse discrimination grievances pending against him, and now this. Why couldn't Mrs. Walker leave it alone? The child would be attending another school in fall. Mr. Clayborn's plate was full and he didn't need more trouble. He knew he had to do something to silence Ella.

* * *

Weeks went by and Ella never heard another word from Mr. Clayborn. Jennifer's behavior towards Bryce had changed though. She hadn't abused him since Ella's meeting with the principal. Jennifer had a different attitude towards Ella. She was quieter and had little to say. When she did talk to Ella, it was condescendingly. She stopped discussing the day's activities with Ella. Ella watched and figured out what was supposed to happen and followed. She guessed Mr. Clayborn told Jennifer she'd been reported. Ella didn't care if Jennifer was angry, as long as she left Bryce alone. Ella was glad she'd seen the principal. She knew she did the right thing.

* * *

Ella was ready to leave for the day when she saw Galen Small, the assistant school librarian, on the stairway.

Galen was a scrawny little man. His height and his weight was about the same as some of the sixth graders at Carter. His thundering mouth made up for his size.

Galen had an obvious hatred for white people. He was a black militant always fighting for a cause. A belligerent bigot, he blamed the white man for everything bad that happened to blacks. He participated in the Million Man March and was disappointed because it turned out peaceful. He was an active member of the (BPA) Black People's Alliance, an organization similar to the Ku Klux Klan, created solely for the purpose of destroying the white man. Galen had been arrested several times for race related incidents.

Mr. Clayborn was not one of Galen's favorite people. He referred to Mr. Clayborn as a sellout because of his interracial marriage. Galen filed a reverse discrimination grievance against Mr. Clayborn when Mr. Clayborn gave the head librarian position to a white employee.

"Hello, Mrs. Walker. You look awfully happy. Could it be because it's only a few days left until summer vacation?"

"Yes, but I'll miss the children."

"Will you lose any of the children to rezoning?"

"Bryce Monday and Maggie Haas."

"Speaking of Bryce, how is the little guy? Is his lip okay?"

"What do you mean, Galen?"

"Well, I wasn't going to say anything, but yesterday I heard scuffling noises on this very same stairway. When I looked around the corner, I saw Ms. Reinhart and Bryce. She had Bryce face down on the stairs. She had his arms behind his back. Bryce tried to scream, but his face was pressed against the stair and his lip was bleeding. Not real bad though, but I could tell she was hurting him."

Upset, Ella asked, "Did you stop her?"

"I yelled at her to quit. She reassured me he wasn't in pain, but I know he was. When she lifted him from the floor, his lip was bleeding. I walked over to Bryce and asked him if he was okay. He smiled. Jennifer said if he was in any real pain he wouldn't be smiling."

Ella folded her arms. "That's bullshit, I hope you didn't believe her."

"I told that big white masculine looking bitch that if I ever saw her do that again, I'd report her ass."

"What did she say?"

"Jennifer told me to stick to my books and leave Bryce to her. I asked her if she treated the white kids in her class like that. She told me that you and her had to restrain Bryce by forcibly holding him down because he had uncontrollable tantrums."

Ella scowled. "That's a damn lie. I would never do that to a child."

"When she told me you and her had to handle Bryce this way, I figured it must be okay. I know he wasn't born right and I don't know how they handle kids like him."

"Jennifer is a liar. If it was okay to treat Bryce this way, why would she immediately stop when she saw you?"

"Funny thing, when she spotted me, she jerked him to his feet, held his hand and started humming *Ring Around The Rosies.*"

CHAPTER FIVE

Beverly Monday watched the clock all afternoon. It was the end of the day, and all she could think about was going home to begin a comfortable and relaxing evening.

Employed by Bertram Group Insurance, Beverly had been with the company for ten years. She originally started as a work experience student and was hired as a permanent employee after she graduated from college. At first she was the office gofer. She filed, answered phones, typed, made copies and kept the office clean until five years ago, when she was promoted to Director of Human Resources.

When Beverly's phone rang at four-thirty, her first instinct was to let her voice mail answer it. She didn't want to take another business call, but at the same time, maybe, it was concerning her son. Perhaps Bryce missed the bus, or, maybe, he was injured. Just the other day Bryce came home with a busted lip. Ms. Reinhart sent a note in his book bag informing her that he had tripped while getting on the bus. Beverly was very protective of Bryce and told Ms. Reinhart to call her immediately when Bryce was hurt and not send a note.

God forbid if it was Mr. Clayborn complaining about Bryce spitting on the bus and threatening suspension if she didn't make him stop.

"Hello, this is Beverly Monday, how can I help you?"

"Hi, Ms. Monday, this is Jennifer Reinhart."

Beverly had asked Ms. Reinhart a million times to call her Beverly and it still hadn't registered.

Worried, she asked, "Is Bryce okay?"

"Oh, yes, he's fine. The kids left school at noon. Only a half-day today. Two more days of school and summer vacation will officially start for Bryce. Actually, I called about myself. I need your help."

"Sure, what can I do?"

"I'd like to come and talk to you this evening. I might need your support on an issue at school."

"What kind of an issue? Does it have anything to do with Bryce?"

"I'd like to discuss this with you in person."

"If it doesn't concern Bryce, then I don't understand."

"I may need you to speak to Mr. Clayborn on my behalf."

"Oh, say no more. When he wanted to suspend Bryce for spitting, it was your intervention that made him realize it wouldn't do any good. I really appreciated that. So, of course, I'll be happy to do whatever you need. I wish you would tell me what the problem is. Maybe, I could take care of this with a phone call to Mr. Clayborn."

"I prefer to discuss it with you in person."

"When would you like to come?"

"How about six o'clock on Friday, if that's convenient?"

"That will be fine." Beverly wrote Ms. Reinhart's name on her calendar. "That'll give me a chance to get something to eat and Bryce settled."

"Okay, I'll see you then. You know, Ms. Monday, I want you to know I really enjoyed having Bryce in my class. I'm going to miss him terribly."

"Well, I'm sure if Bryce could talk, he would tell you he feels the same way. I know I do. I'm not looking forward to Bryce going to another school. You know, getting used to the teacher, the handicapped children's assistant and the other children. Sure you don't want to transfer to Palmer? It would be great to have you as my son's teacher again."

"That's nice of you to feel that way. Thanks for the compliment."

"Well, Ms. Reinhart, I have the utmost respect for your profession, and you as a person."

"Thank you. I really appreciate your willingness to help me."

"Sure, no problem. Whatever I can do to help. I'll see you at six o'clock on Friday."

* * *

Mr. Clayborn was about to turn the light switch off when Ella appeared at his office.

"Did you talk to Jennifer Reinhart?"

"Mrs. Walker, it's been a long day, can't this wait until tomorrow?"

Ella walked past Mr. Clayborn and stood in the middle of his office.

"It's been five weeks since I first talked to you. No, it can't wait until tomorrow."

Mr. Clayborn sighed and closed the door. "I know I told you I would meet with Jennifer Reinhart and Beverly Monday...."

Ella interrupted. "I'm really glad because Jennifer shouldn't get away with this."

"Wait, Mrs. Walker. You misunderstand."

He walked over to his desk and sat down.

"Please, have a seat."

Firmly, Ella said, "I think I'll stand. What do you mean, I misunderstood?"

"I talked to Ms. Reinhart and told her about your concern and she feels you have a problem with her as an authority figure because she's younger than you. I told her I was going to schedule a meeting with the three of us and Beverly Monday. She is in total agreement of this meeting with Ms. Monday."

"Well, good because when I tell Ms. Monday what Jennifer's been doing to Bryce, I don't think she'll be so agreeable."

"I'm not going to contact Ms. Monday. I've decided against having a meeting."

Shocked, Ella asked, "Why not?" She moved closer to Mr. Clayborn's desk and sat in the chair across from him.

"I saw Ms. Reinhart again on the floor with Bryce. I, too, was concerned. She, however, guaranteed me that her grip was perfectly safe and was not painful to the child. Ms. Reinhart also assured me he was screaming only because it's merely a ploy to be released.

Ella cried, "You bought that?" She pushed her chair back from the desk and stood. "I can't believe you. If you heard and saw Bryce screaming then you witnessed her abusing him. Believe your eyes, Mr. Clayborn. You saw what she did."

Mr. Clayborn stood. "Look, I know this child, and he can be uncontrollable. I've already called his mother on several occasions because he was spitting. I told her I was going to suspend him if it happened again. It was Ms. Reinhart who spoke up on his behalf."

"Mr. Clayborn, he's eight years old, but, mentally, he's about nine months. You should've known he wouldn't understand a suspension."

"Mrs. Walker, I don't need your sarcasm. The bottom line is I don't feel Ms. Reinhart is doing anything wrong. I informed her there wouldn't be a meeting with Ms. Monday."

"You don't think it's wrong for her to call the kids retards?"

"This school is fortunate to have Ms. Reinhart. Just because she's a little behind time and she still refers to cognitively disabled children as retarded doesn't mean she's abusive."

Ella frowned.

"Look, school has officially ended for summer vacation. Bryce will be going to another school in fall. Please don't make an issue of this."

Ella started towards the door. "I'm sorry I ever thought I could get your help. If Jennifer was black and Bryce white, you'd do something. Wouldn't you?"

"Mrs. Walker, I want this to end right here. Don't make trouble for me. I have enough to deal with. I still have the reverse discrimination grievances hanging over my head. I mean it, don't make something out of nothing."

Ella rolled her eyes and pointed her finger at Mr. Clayborn. "This is very much something and if you don't care, I do." She opened the door, walked out.

"Mrs. Walker," Mr. Clayborn yelled after her. "Your six month review is coming up, isn't it? I can't tell you how many qualified applicants applied for your job."

Ella turned around. She eyeballed Mr. Clayborn, but did not respond. She left and closed the door behind her.

* * *

On June 7, Ella received her six-month evaluation from Jennifer Reinhart and Robert Clayborn. She was rated poorly. The evaluation was the worse she'd received in twenty years.

* * *

That same evening Beverly picked up Bryce from her sister's and went home.

Beverly arrived home around six o'clock, and had started to prepare dinner when the phone rang. It was Jennifer Reinhart.

"Hi, Ms. Monday. I just called to tell you that I won't be able to meet with you tomorrow evening."

"Okay. Would you like to reschedule? I'm flexible."

"No. As a matter of fact I settled everything so I won't need to meet with you after all."

"Are you sure?"

"Yes."

"What was it about anyway?"

"It's not even worth mentioning." Jennifer said.

"Okay," Beverly said. "Are you sure you don't want to tell me what was going on at school?"

"It's over and done with." Jennifer said. "Oh, I almost forgot to mention that today was Bryce's last day of school. Tomorrow's a half-day of school. There's no need to send Bryce. I informed the other parents, too. Listen, you and Bryce have a nice summer and good luck at Palmer Elementary."

* * *

Ella saw Agnes Harris, the third grade teacher, in her classroom straightening up before going home.

Agnes was a religious woman. She attended church on Sundays and Bible study on Wednesday night. The Bible was her reference book. She lived by it and would probably die by it. At fifty-nine, Agnes was a huge black woman. Her over-active sweat glands, at times, generated an unpleasant scent. She never married and lived alone in a one-bedroom apartment.

Agnes, also, filed a grievance against Robert Clayborn. Mr. Clayborn prevented Agnes from teaching the children in her class about the Bible, but allowed a white teacher to teach prayers to her students.

"Agnes, can I talk to you for a minute?" Ella asked.

"Sure. I'm just organizing the room so it'll be ready for me in September. We made it through another school year. The children have a half-day of school tomorrow, so as far as I'm concerned, this is it. Do you have big plans for the summer?"

"No. Agnes, I'm really upset."

Agnes stopped organizing the books on her desk and looked at Ella. "What's wrong?"

"I reported Jennifer Reinhart to Mr. Clayborn because she's been physically abusing Bryce and because of that I got a horrible review."

Agnes rubbed her temple with her index finger. "I saw Ms. Reinhart squeeze his hand with both of hers once."

Surprised, Ella asked, "When?"

"About a week ago, Ms. Reinhart and Bryce were coming from the gym. I think you'd left to take Maggie to her mom because she picked her up early that day from school. You were only gone for a few minutes."

"Yes, I remember. Tell me what happened?"

"I suppose Bryce wasn't walking fast enough because his feet kept getting tangled. Probably because he's so pigeon-toed. Ms.

Reinhart grabbed Bryce's hand and squeezed it. Bryce moaned because it hurt. I could tell Ms. Reinhart was applying pressure because she was biting down on her bottom lip and her face was distorted."

"Did you stop her?"

"When she noticed me, she released the pressure and started humming *Ring Around The Rosies* to the poor child as if nothing was wrong."

* * *

On June 8, the last day of school, Ella Walker filed a grievance with the president of the Melbourne Teacher's Union for the unfair performance review she received.

On the same day, Ella Walker, Galen Small and Agnes Harris submitted written statements to the union describing how they witnessed Jennifer Reinhart's abuse of Bryce Monday.

* * *

Beverly left work Friday evening, picked Bryce up from her sister, Sharon, and stopped for burgers. They arrived home around six o'clock.

Beverly and Bryce finished eating around six-fifty. She gave Bryce a bath and read him a story. Bryce liked being in water, so bath time was a fun time. Slightly clumsy because of his pigeon toes, Beverly had to be extra watchful of him. Sometimes he would trip and bump himself. He bruised easily. He once bruised his back because the buckle on his book bag pressed into his back while on the bus. She bought him one without buckles.

She put Bryce to bed and minutes later he was asleep. It was about nine, when she decided to relax with a glass of wine and the phone rang.

"Ms. Monday, my name is Jeffrey Garrison. I'm president of the teacher's union. I'm calling in regard to your son, Bryce."

"What about my son?" she questioned.

"I really don't want to get into it over the phone. I was wondering if you could come to my office."

"Not without knowing what's going on."

"Ms. Monday, I received several written statements from employees at Carter. These statements describe how Bryce Monday was physically abused by his teacher, Jennifer Reinhart."

CHAPTER SIX

Jeffrey Garrison has been the president of the teacher's union for Melbourne Public School System for four years. He had negotiated excellent wages for the teachers and won many grievances. Talking to the mother of an abused child was the hardest thing Mr. Garrison had ever had to do in this position. He read the statements over and over, and the horror of it was unbelievable.

He drank his coffee and waited patiently for Beverly Monday. His dinky office was located in Valley Office Park. Reluctantly, it was rented by Melbourne Public School System after numerous complaints from Mr. Garrison that he had nowhere to meet with union members to discuss union issues.

* * *

Beverly had not planned on spending Saturday morning listening to what probably was a mistake. She called her sister, Sharon, who agreed to watch Bryce.

Sharon Edwards was Beverly's younger sister. They were very close. Being only two years apart, people sometimes had a hard time telling who was the eldest.

They were best friends. They did everything together growing up. Neither of them had very many friends because they had each other. People sometimes thought they were twins when they were younger because their mother dressed them alike. Sometimes they would lie and tell people they were.

Sharon was a registered nurse. She worked the night shift and during the day she kept Bryce. The school bus would drop Bryce off after school, and during the summer he would stay with Sharon while Beverly was at work.

Aside from being his aunt, she was his godmother. Sharon was fond of Bryce. Beverly knew if she wasn't around, Sharon would take care of Bryce.

Sharon was married to Tyler. Tyler was a supervisor at Wisconsin Construction Company.

The couple didn't have any children together. Tyler had a son from a previous relationship. He never really wanted children and had a vasectomy after his son was born.

Sharon and Tyler lived about ten minutes from Beverly. Beverly arrived at eight-forty. She parked in front of Sharon's house and started to walk Bryce to the door. Sharon stood in the doorway and greeted them.

"Hey, Bryce." Sharon said and took his hand. Bryce flapped his other hand and jumped up and down like he was going to fly. His grin revealed all his white teeth.

Sharon smiled. "I know what that means." Sharon picked Bryce up and hugged him. She tickled him under his arm and kissed him on the cheek, then on top of his head. Bryce giggled. He rubbed Sharon's dark brown cheeks.

"Thanks for watching Bryce. I shouldn't be gone long."

"Don't you have time to come in? I made coffee."

"No. I'll be back as soon as possible."

Beverly turned around and went back to her car and left.

* * *

Jeffrey Garrison's office was located just north of Sharon's house. Dressed in a navy jogging suit, Beverly arrived shortly after nine a.m. She felt nervous as she bit her pinky nail down to the skin. Beverly sighed, then knocked on the door.

"Are you Mr. Garrison?" Beverly asked.

Mr. Garrison was clean shaven. He had short brown hair with a hint of gray. He wore tennis shoes and a white tee-shirt that had

Wisconsin—A Great State across the front in black letters that was neatly tucked in his black jeans. He cleared his throat. "You must be Beverly Monday?"

Beverly nodded.

"Come in and have a seat." He pointed to the chair at his desk. "Please, call me Jeffrey. "May I get you a cup of coffee?"

Beverly gripped her purse tightly with both of her sweaty hands and said, "No thanks. Just tell me what's going on with my son. Your phone call frightened me." Her voice trembled.

"Ms. Monday, I received a letter from Ella Walker."

Beverly, interrupted. "That's the aide in my son's class."

"Yes. Mrs. Walker wrote me because she had reported Jennifer Reinhart to the principal regarding the way she was handling Bryce. She felt Ms. Reinhart was too rough and, at times, caused him tremendous pain. Mrs. Walker contacted me when the principal failed to reprimand Ms. Reinhart."

"I don't believe this. Ms. Reinhart would never hurt Bryce. She is always pleasant and nice. Is this some kind of sick joke?"

"Absolutely not, I would never joke about something as serious as this. Never."

Beverly stood.

"Before you leave, I have to tell you everything. I know you care about your child, otherwise, you wouldn't have come."

Beverly sat down. "You're right. I love my son very much and I wouldn't be here if I didn't care. Do you believe Mrs. Walker?"

"Yes, Ma'am, I do. In fact, when she discussed this with other teachers, it was acknowledged others had witnessed Ms. Reinhart's use of excessive force on Bryce."

"My God." Beverly's heart beat faster. "What kind of force? How did she abuse him? Did she hit him?"

"I have three handwritten statements," he handed her the papers, "by three individuals who witnessed the abuse."

Beverly moved closer to the edge of her chair. Her hands trembled. Quietly, she asked, "Who else?"

"One statement is signed by Mrs. Walker, the other one by the Librarian, Galen Small, and another teacher named Agnes Harris."

"I know Mr. Small. He always said hello to me and Bryce when I used to visit Bryce's class while I was on a leave of absence from work. I don't know Agnes Harris."

"Ms. Harris is the third grade teacher."

"I don't understand how this could have happened. I was on a leave of absence from work. My mother died and I took four months off work to straighten out her affairs. I made unannounced visits all the time and never saw anything happening in the classroom to make me feel my child was in danger."

"You read what they wrote and decide. I felt it was my duty to tell you. Especially since the principal didn't do anything."

Beverly read the first statement from Ella Walker and felt sick to her stomach.

She read the next statement from Galen Small. Tears stung her eyes. The paper shook in her trembling hands. Beverly couldn't speak. She took a deep breath and read the last statement from Agnes Harris.

All the while, Mr. Garrison sat in his chair, sipped his coffee.

Beverly wiped the tears from her eyes and shook her head as she read the last statement. She started to read out loud. "Bryce screamed in pain." She swallowed hard and looked up at Mr. Garrison.

Mr. Garrison asked, "Are you okay?"

She squeezed the papers with her hand and shook them at Mr. Garrison. "How can this be?" Beverly shivered. "I don't understand."

Beverly put the statements on the desk, pushed her chair back and stood.

"Why would Jennifer Reinhart hurt Bryce? Why would she hurt my son?"

Mr. Garrison stood. "I don't know why anyone would ever harm a child. I think it is the sickest of all crimes."

Beverly walked over to the desk, picked up the statements again, paged through them before she tossed them back on the desk.

Mr. Garrison handed her a tissue. Beverly collapsed in the chair.

"This is incredible, Mr. Garrison. All the visits and conversations with Ms. Reinhart, how could I have not known? Mrs. Walker never said a word to me. No one has ever indicated that Bryce was in danger. Ms. Reinhart has always shown tenderness towards my son."

Trembling, Beverly wiped her tears and blew her nose. "That just doesn't sound like someone who's doing something wrong. I mean, when I told her I was going back to work, she even told me she would really miss my visits." Beverly added.

"Again, Ms. Monday, I only wanted to let you know about these statements." He handed her the papers. "These are yours to keep. I don't know if you want to show these to an attorney or not. But if you need me, here's my card, give me a call."

Beverly stood as she took the card, thanked Mr. Garrison and left.

When Beverly reached her car, she paged through the statements once again. She threw them on the dash board, grabbed the steering wheel and cried profusely. She couldn't believe this was happening. She was mad and scared. She trusted Jennifer. She wondered how she could do this to her son.

Beverly thought about her parents and wished they were alive. They would know what to do. She was angry at herself because if Bryce was abused, she should have known.

She went to Sharon's to get Bryce and decided not to say a word about her meeting with Mr. Garrison. How could she tell her sister, someone who loved Bryce as much as she did, that he'd been abused. Sharon would flip. If she didn't do anything about it, then she wouldn't have to tell Sharon. After all, Bryce would attend a different school in fall so he never had to deal with Jennifer again.

It was about eleven-fifteen when Beverly arrived at Sharon's front door.

"Hey, Sis. That didn't take long at all. Is everything okay?" Sharon asked.

"Sure, where's Bryce?"

"He's watching cartoons with Tyler."

Beverly came in and stood in the middle of the living room. She scanned the green plants that surrounded the room. She noticed

Bryce's toy truck on the brown velvet sofa. She glanced at the picture of Sharon on the cherrywood end table.

Beverly couldn't look directly at Sharon. She might be able to tell something was wrong. She would get Bryce and leave quickly before Sharon could ask questions or sense something was wrong. She had to play it cool.

"Would you get Bryce for me, Sharon. We're going grocery shopping and I want to stop and get Bryce some summer outfits. I have a feeling it's going to be a hot one."

"Girl, please, a hot summer in Melbourne, Wisconsin? I don't think so. Maybe, one or two days, but that's it." Sharon laughed.

"It's not even noon and I heard on the radio that it's already seventy-three degrees." Beverly said.

"Honey," Sharon yelled to Tyler, "bring Bryce out. Bev's here."

"I should go with you and Bryce," Sharon said. "I need to buy myself some new shoes and uniforms for work. But I think I'll stay home because I really need to clean this house. This is the first weekend I've had off in ages. This place is saying, stop being so lazy and clean me."

Sharon laughed and Beverly pretended to join in.

Tyler entered the room with Bryce. Tyler was muscular. His quarter of an inch afro was neatly lined and his goatee perfectly trimmed.

"Hey, Beverly, how's it going?" Tyler said.

"Oh, it's going. How are you Tyler?" Beverly asked.

"Not bad for an old man."

Bryce walked over to Beverly and she kneeled down and hugged him. "Are you ready, big guy? I'm going to buy your favorite cereal. I'm also going to buy you some summer clothes today. How about that?"

Beverly stood, stroking Bryce's curly hair. She looked at Tyler. "I know he doesn't understand."

"You keep on talking to him," Tyler said. "He understands more than you think."

Sharon walked over to Bryce and kneeled.

"Of course, you do." Sharon hugged him tightly and kissed him on the forehead. "This is what tells you you're loved a lot and I know you understand."

Bryce smiled.

"Thanks, guys. I gotta go," Beverly said.

"Take care Beverly and you too, my main man. Give me five." Tyler extended his hand, palm up. Bryce slapped five.

Amazed, Beverly asked, "Oh my goodness, where did he learn to do that?"

"I taught him." Tyler said proudly. "I told you, Bryce knows a lot more than you think."

Beverly thought about her visit with Mr. Garrison and wondered if Bryce did understand more than she realized. If that were true, then how could he have been abused? But Bryce couldn't speak and Beverly knew there was no way he could tell.

Beverly and Bryce headed for the car, Sharon followed. Beverly could fool everybody but Sharon. Beverly knew Sharon suspected something was wrong and she knew it had to do with Beverly's appointment this morning.

Beverly sat Bryce in the front seat and put his seat belt on. She proceeded around the car to the driver's side.

Sharon followed and stopped her at the back of the car. "Beverly, wait a minute." She grabbed her wrist. "Talk to me. Tell me what's going on?"

"Nothing Sharon. I gotta go."

"Look, you can fool everybody but me. You just can't. So you might as well tell me. I know something's wrong and I know it has something to do with your appointment this morning."

"I can't discuss this in front of Bryce. I'll call you later." She hugged Sharon.

"All right, you better. Because you know if you don't, I'm going to call you. Bev, we're all we've got now that Mama's gone."

Beverly got in the car and drove off.

* * *

Beverly and Bryce spent the whole day shopping. They went to several stores in the mall and finally ended up at the toy store.

There was nothing abnormal about Bryce when it came to the toy store. He was every bit as excited and loved toys like any other eight-year-old boy. He could not verbalize his desires, but he sure knew how to get his point across. He would wrap his arms around the toy and wouldn't give it to Beverly. She knew that was the toy he wanted.

Bryce chose a police truck with a siren. He was always drawn to toys that made loud noises.

Beverly stood in the long line to pay for the toy. Too bad there wasn't more than one cashier. There was no way she could come back another day for the toy. Bryce would probably have a tantrum and she didn't need the attention. Besides, Bryce had already gone through enough with his teacher. It wasn't so bad and Beverly was in no hurry to go outside in the heat. She stood in line with Bryce and enjoyed the air-conditioning.

Beverly watched Bryce holding the car. Should she call the police and report the abuse? Maybe, if she showed them the written statements, they could advise her.

Angry and confused, Beverly thought about confronting Jennifer Reinhart. She'd have to wait till fall when school started. She had no idea where Jennifer lived or how to get in touch with her.

Why hadn't the other teachers called the police? All the visits she made to the school and no one never let on anything bad was going on. Maybe, the teachers were the ones she should confront. Surely, Mr. Garrison knew how to get in touch with them.

Tears burned her eyes. She had to organize her thoughts. There was nothing she could do right now anyway.

A cashier called from the express lane. "This register is open. I can help someone over here." Beverly took Bryce's hand and scurried over to the next cashier. In a matter of minutes, Beverly and her son were out the door. The temperature had reached a sweltering ninety-eight degrees.

She glanced at her watch. She hadn't realized it was after five. Hungry, she stopped for pizza before heading home.

* * *

Sharon spent the whole day cleaning her house from top to bottom. She cleaned every corner. She waxed and mopped the kitchen floor. She dusted, polished and shined every picture, table and crystal in the house. With her hectic schedule at the hospital, Sharon knew it would be a while, maybe, even months before she had another weekend off, so this cleaning had to last for a while.

Sharon tried calling her sister several times and kept getting her voice mail. She left a message each time, but still no return call.

Sharon knew her sister. Whenever Beverly was really troubled about something she became withdrawn. When Sharon and Beverly were children, Beverly would stay in her room all day. She never wanted to bother anyone with her problems. Sharon would always reassure her that you're not bothering family when you share a problem. It was her reassurance that always made Beverly finally open up.

Sharon was positive Beverly was upset about something. She stared out the kitchen window. Tyler was mowing the lawn. She thought about asking him if he noticed anything about Beverly's behavior, but decided not to. It was best to wait until she talked to Beverly.

Sharon finished with her cleaning by six-thirty. She showered and decided cooking was the last thing she wanted to do. She talked Tyler into going out for dinner.

* * *

After Beverly and Bryce finished dinner, Beverly let Bryce watch the cartoon channel. Whoever came up with the idea to have a television channel dedicated to nothing but cartoons must have children, probably a lot of children. Bryce sat on the floor in front of the television, holding his new toy. Beverly was on the couch and went through her mail. She ignored the flashing red light on her answering machine as long as she could. She knew it was Sharon.

Sharon had left the same message three times: "Hey, Sis, it's me. Give me a call when you get in."

Beverly knew she had to call her. She needed to tell Sharon. Maybe, together they could make some sense out of this. She decided to call after she'd finished reading her mail.

* * *

It was about ten o'clock when Sharon and Tyler returned from dinner. Sharon immediately checked the messages, only one call for Tyler from a prospective client.

Tyler yawned. "I'm tired, I'll call him tomorrow. I think I'll watch television in bed."

Sharon decided to try calling Beverly again. She was beginning to get upset. She really thought Beverly would have returned her call by now. Beverly answered on the third ring.

"Girl, I was about to hang up and come over there. What took you so long to come to the phone. Why haven't you called me?"

"I was putting Bryce to bed and I was going to call you after that."

"I want to know what's going on right now."

Beverly started sniffling and Sharon knew she was crying. "Why are you crying? Is it Bryce? Is he okay?"

"My baby's fine now."

"What do you mean by fine now?"

Beverly cried louder. "Oh God, Sharon, I'm so upset. I just don't know what to do."

"Do about what? I know this has something to do with your meeting today."

Beverly was crying and breathing fast.

"For God's sake, Beverly, tell me. You're scaring me. Just say it."

Still breathing fast and crying out loud, Beverly finally said, "I found out that Bryce's teacher abused him over and over."

Sharon released the receiver and it fell in her lap.

CHAPTER SEVEN

Inez Connors was awakened by her alarm every morning at five a.m. After dressing, she jogged to the square and back. On her return home, she worked out in the gym she'd created in her spare bedroom. She spent twenty minutes each on her bike, treadmill, followed by aerobics. After her shower, she watched the early morning news while having a cup of black coffee with cream.

She lived in Beaver Point, about five miles north of Melbourne, in a beautiful Lannon Stone, one story, three bedroom Tudor home, that she purchased two years ago. The house was five minutes from the freeway and was a straight shot to her office.

The natural hardwood floors, the fireplace in the living room and the stained glass windows in the formal dining room was well worth her mortgage payment of $1,150 per month.

An only child, Inez was thirty-eight. Her parents lived in Arizona. She talked to them three times a week and visited for two weeks every summer.

She was widowed at age twenty-seven when her husband, Allen, and nine-month-old daughter, Allie, were killed in a car accident by a drunk driver. After nine months of mourning and deep depression, she joined MADD, Mothers Against Drunk Drivers, to help fill the void in her life.

When the legal system gave the driver who killed her family three years probation and treatment for alcoholism as an outpatient; and when she saw the number of mothers who had lost children unnecessarily to intoxicated drivers, she decided to divert her career from that of a bankruptcy attorney to criminal law. Her long term plan was to become a judge in family court.

Inez taught Sunday school to pre-teens. Inez loved children, but never wanted any more because of her fear of losing another. She decided it was best to help the children who were already in the world.

She never remarried and only dated men who had children. She broke up with her last beau, David, because even though he paid his child support faithfully, he never spent any time with his children.

Inez was an emotional person. She was compassionate and empathetic to the pain of her clients. If she didn't have faith in her clients, she wouldn't take the case.

About a year ago, Inez handled a case against a slum landlord. Her client, twenty-five-year-old Daphne Rogers repeatedly complained about the unsafe conditions in the apartment, that she and her three year-old-son, Jamal, rented from George Dumas. The apartment was loaded with code violations, leaking faucets, no smoke alarms, cracked and peeling ceilings, to name a few.

Daphne, along with other tenants in the building, were unsuccessful in their numerous attempts to get Mr. Dumas to budge from his grand Colonial home in upper Melbourne. One day the ceiling in the living room caved in and fell on Jamal, fracturing his spine, leaving him permanently paralyzed from the waist down.

Inez sued Mr. Dumas, and through his insurance, Inez collected three and a half million dollars for her client. The case was on television and made the front page of the newspaper.

When Inez finished her breakfast she went upstairs to her bedroom. She opened her walk-in closet and pulled out her black suit. She shook her head, hung the suit back in the closet and pulled out her two piece yellow and white suit. She decided that would be more appropriate for the sultry weather.

She slipped into her size eight outfit and slid into her white three inch pumps.

She maneuvered her shoulder-length dark brown hair into a french roll and secured it with a pearl comb. She pulled out a few strands of hair on each side and full bangs in the front. She curled them loosely with electric curlers.

She covered her caramel colored skin with make-up, put on her fuschia lipstick and her pearl-drop earrings.

Inez drove a 1997 royal blue Benz that was under a two year lease at a whopping $600 per month. She preferred leasing, that way, she would always ride in something new and dependable.

Vehicular movement was congested, bumper-to-bumper, during rush hour. Inez listened to the jazz station on the radio while she patiently waited in traffic.

Her office was located in downtown Melbourne in the Foster Plankinton Building on the fifth floor, suite five hundred. Two floors below her office, suite three hundred, was the Jordan Medical Clinic that religiously performed abortions. Inez, along with her paralegal, Joey Miles, rented the office space three years ago. A year ago she created a partnership with Martin Townsend, becoming The Law Offices of Connors and Townsend.

The office was divided into sections. The entrance was an area designated for the receptionist, Connie, which Inez and her law partner shared. Connie was light-skinned with short black hair. Down the hall to the left was her partner's office, and Inez's was to the right. The two rooms in the middle were used as a library and a conference room.

"Good Morning, Connie."

Her secretary paused, her fingers poised above the keyboard of her computer. "Morning. I won't say good though."

"Yes, I know. Mondays are always a hassle around here. Any messages?"

"Only two." She handed them to Inez. "A message from Attorney Phillip Quinn. I think he wants to settle."

Attorney Quinn was Inez's opponent in a dispute over the adoption of a three-year-old baby girl. When it was learned the mother was a drug addict, the court placed the child with a foster family when she was only a month old. The couple came to Inez to petition the court to legally adopt the child and forever ban the mother from seeking custody. When the mother learned of the plan, she hired Quinn.

When Inez unequivocally established that the mother was still using drugs, Attorney Quinn thought it best not to risk his client losing all of her parental rights, but play it safe and settle for supervised visits. Inez would settle out of court, but decided to let Attorney Quinn sweat for a while.

"And the second message," Connie said, "is from your MADD group."

"What about appointments? What's scheduled for me today?" Inez asked.

"You have an eleven-fifteen appointment with a woman name Beverly Monday. She didn't say what it was about. Oh, and Mable Murray will be in at two-thirty to set up trusts for her two children."

Mable Murray was the beneficiary to her father's life insurance policy. Mable collected $750,000 when her father died. She wanted to set up trusts for her children, two-year-old Ann and Craig, six. She was afraid that if something happened to her, their frivolous father, Luke, would squander the money.

Inez went to her office.

* * *

Beverly felt fortunate to promptly get an appointment with Inez Connors. Sharon suggested Inez because she remembered reading about her slum landlord case last year in the newspaper. She recalled the live interview after the trial and how Inez cried because even though her client won, Inez stated no dollar amount was enough to replace the use of the little boy's legs.

Sharon was astonished at the compassion and the heartfelt sympathy that Inez showed for her client.

Beverly took Bryce to Sharon's around ten-forty-five a.m. She was nervous about her meeting and Sharon knew it. Bryce grinned broadly at the sight of Sharon. He ran toward her. Sharon caught him before he stumbled over his feet. "Hey Bryce. I'm glad to see you too, Sweetie." Sharon picked him up and hugged him. She kissed him on his cheek. Bryce cooed.

Sharon hugged Bryce tighter, and stroked Beverly's shoulder. "Are you going to be okay? I could go with you. If you don't want to take Bryce, Tyler will watch him."

"No, I'll be fine. Thanks for helping me find an attorney." Sharon and Bryce walked Beverly to the door. Beverly kissed Bryce and left.

* * *

When Beverly arrived, the sidewalk in front of the office building was packed with picketers. At least fifty anti-abortionists paced in the front carrying signs.

Beverly was nervous. She had to go through the crowd and be thought upon as a killer. She was sure the picketers would think she was going to the clinic for an abortion.

She started through the crowd, but a man holding a sign that read, *Abortion Kills* blocked her way.

The man yelled, "How can you kill your child? Have you no decency?"

Beverly pushed past him, but was shoved by a woman carrying a sign that read, *Thou Shalt Not Kill.*

The woman grabbed Beverly by the arm. "Don't go in there. There're other alternatives. Your baby deserves a chance at life."

Furious, Beverly jerked away. "Let go of me," she yelled. "How dare you assume I'm here for an abortion. There are other businesses in this building. I resent your accusation, and even if I was going for an abortion, it's none of your damn business. Who in the hell do you think you are?"

"May I ask where you're going?" The woman questioned.

"Not that it's any of your business, but I have an appointment at the law office."

The woman reached in her purse and handed Beverly a brochure. "May I give you this? It's a brochure that describes how abortions are performed."

Beverly took the brochure and paged through it. There were gruesome pictures of aborted fetuses. The heads of fetuses severed, arms ripped away from their tiny bodies. Beverly was shocked. "I can't believe this takes place when a woman has an abortion."

"Then you disagree with abortion? Would you like to support our cause and march with us?" The woman asked.

"I didn't say I agreed or disagreed with abortion. Don't put words in my mouth." Beverly plowed her way through the crowd until she was inside the building. She passed a woman on her way to the elevator and found herself guilty of the same conclusion about her that the protestors had assumed about her.

When Beverly arrived, Connie immediately informed Inez. Connie escorted Beverly to the conference room.

Beverly sat in an oak chair at the round oak table in the center of the rectangle room. There was a phone at the head of the table. Tan wallpaper with a dark brown border covered the walls. There was an eleven by seventeen picture of a law library on the wall facing the head of the table, a round silver trimmed clock on the wall on the left and a five feet rubber tree in each corner.

When Inez entered, she carried a pen and yellow legal pad of paper in her hand. "Beverly Monday? I'm Inez Connors." They shook hands.

"Nice to meet you, Ms. Connors." Inez sat next to Beverly. "I apologize for not seeing you in my office. I have papers all over my desk and floor because I'm trying to prepare for an upcoming case."

Beverly glanced at Inez. "No problem." She said.

"So, how can I help you, Ms. Monday?"

"I received a call from a man by the name of Jeffrey Garrison, president of the teacher's union for Melbourne Public School System, regarding my son. I went to his office last Saturday morning." Beverly reached in her purse and pulled out the three statements and handed them to Inez. "He gave me these statements and that's what brought me to you."

Inez read the statements one at a time, frowning. "Who in the hell is this woman and what is she doing around children?"

"First of all, Ms. Connors, I think I should tell you my son is eight-years-old. He is cognitively disabled and nonverbal."

"All the more reason he shouldn't be treated like this." Inez slammed the statements on the table, stood up and paced the office with one hand on her hip. "The principal did nothing?" Inez asked. "I don't believe it."

Tears stung Beverly's eyes. "I know. I just can't believe that this was going on right under my nose and I didn't even know it. I told Mr. Garrison I was on a leave of absence from work and made numerous unannounced visits to Bryce's classroom. Jennifer Reinhart encouraged the visits. When I informed her I would be returning to work, she said she would miss me coming to class. That doesn't sound like a person who would abuse my son."

"How long were you on a leave of absence?" Inez asked.

"My Mom died in November, and I was off work from November until February. Why?"

Inez picked up Ella Walker's statement. "Mrs. Walker wrote that the first time Jennifer Reinhart abused Bryce was in March. Ms. Reinhart knew there'd be no more unannounced visits from you because you informed her when you returned to work. Coincidence?" Inez shook her head. "I think not."

Beverly lowered her head, she trembled. "Stupid me. I didn't even realize. How could I be so naïve?"

Inez sat beside Beverly. She put her hand on Beverly's shoulder. "Don't cry. You had no way of knowing. This must be really hard for you. Where's Bryce now?"

"He's with my sister."

Beverly retrieved a tissue from her purse and wiped her eyes. "My sister told me about you. She said you're the best there is. Can you help me? What should I do?"

"No, it's not what you should do, it's what we should do. I say we go after the entire school system. I say we make them holy and sue the hell out of those bastards."

* * *

After Beverly left, Inez remained in the conference room and paged through the statements again. She was amazed at how this could have happened for so long. She wondered why it took so long for the abuse to be reported. Inez thought about her own child and how devastated she was when she died. She understood Beverly's pain.

One thing Inez knew for sure was that she was determined to make all parties involved pay for what happened to this woman's child.

* * *

Beverly was on her way out of the office when a deep soft masculine voice called to her.

"Beverly. Beverly Monday is that you?"

CHAPTER EIGHT

When Attorney Douglas Pratt received a call from Mora Abernathy, Director of Human Resources in the Special Education Division at Melbourne Public School System, he knew, whatever, the problem was, it meant big bucks for him.

Although Douglas was well-known as an excellent attorney, he was once referred to by an opponent as an arrogant, conceited and egotistical bastard.

His piercing voice corresponded with his physique. He was tall and slender for his height. It didn't take much to maintain his one hundred sixty-five pounds. He prided himself on his appearance. His short blond hair complimented his hazel eyes. His clean shaven face gave him a much younger look.

Douglas was a neat freak. Everything had a place, so there was no excuse for anything to be out of place. He was meticulous and raised his sons the same way. He wore nothing but the best suits and shoes, nails manicured once a week and a pedicure twice a month.

He took pride in destroying his opponents in the courtroom. Douglas was good and showed no mercy for anyone, which is probably the reason why Melbourne Public School System retained his services six months after he began his own private law practice.

He hadn't lost any of the four law suits filed against Melbourne Public School System in the six years he worked for them. Douglas was proud of his record and didn't mind letting everyone know it. Life couldn't be better.

His career treated him well. Right after law school he worked for the Law Offices of Masters and Zion. He was assigned to handle several cases for Melbourne Public School System. His law firm,

Law Offices of Douglas Pratt, has been in existence for fifteen years. The firm, located on Griffin Avenue, consisted of Douglas and a part-time secretary.

He was forty-six and his wife, Lynn, was a successful real estate broker. Married for twenty-five years, they had two sons, Douglas, Jr. twelve and Elliot eight.

The Pratts lived in Black Deer, Wisconsin in a two-story Colonial home, which he purchased ten years ago. The four bedrooms, two and a half baths was situated on a beautifully landscaped acre of land. The ceilings in the living and formal dining rooms were Cathedral and both had natural fireplaces. Douglas had a patio deck in the backyard with an in-ground swimming pool, which got very little use in Wisconsin. Ten months out of the year it was cold, but Douglas was known by his neighbors as Mr. Show-and-Tell because he had no problems flaunting his accomplishments.

Douglas showered quickly and was dressed by seven-thirty a.m. His sons were leaving for camp today and he definitely wanted to see them before they left. As he came downstairs, he could smell bacon frying in the kitchen.

Lynn was fixing waffles, eggs and bacon. Douglas, Jr. poked at his eggs with his fork. Elliot sat at the kitchen table, swinging his leg against his suitcase and camping gear, which created a thumping noise.

The boys were finishing their breakfast when Douglas entered the room. "Good morning. Hmm-hmm, something smells good."

"Hello, Father," Elliot said.

"Good Morning, Father," Douglas, Jr. followed.

Lynn was at the stove and had just taken the last of the bacon out of the skillet and brought it to the table.

"Have a seat, Honey, everything's ready. I made yours when I heard you in the shower. I wanted it to be nice and hot."

Douglas walked over to the counter and poured a cup of coffee and he and Lynn sat at the table. His long legs brushed against his son's camping gear and suitcases.

The school bus pulled up and the driver started to blow the horn. The boys quickly got up from the table and grabbed their gear and luggage.

Every summer Douglas, Jr. and Elliot went to camp for four weeks in Dells, Wisconsin. Dells was a five hour drive from Black Deer. Many of the youths who attended Hillsboro went to this camp. Elliot looked forward to camp every summer, but Douglas, Jr. wasn't happy about going this year. He'd developed an interest in girls and wanted to stay home instead of being around a group of boys.

"I hope this is my last year for camp," Douglas, Jr. mumbled as he and Elliot headed for the door.

"We'll talk about it, son." Douglas said.

"Try to have fun, Honey." Lynn kissed them both.

Douglas and Lynn walked to the bus and watched the bus drive out of sight. They returned to the breakfast table.

"Honey, I really don't have time for breakfast. I have a meeting this morning at eight-thirty with Melbourne Public School System. Sorry you went to all this trouble with breakfast, but coffee and juice is all I have time for."

"That's okay. I'll eat it." She grabbed the two strips of bacon off the platter. "Douglas, maybe we should've allowed Douglas, Jr. to stay home after all. He really didn't want to go. He seems so unhappy."

"This camp cost three thousand dollars and there was no way we'd get a refund this late. I have to go to work."

Douglas took another sip of his coffee and gulped down his juice. He kissed Lynn on her cheek. "See you this evening." He grabbed his briefcase and left. He tossed his briefcase inside his recently purchased black Lexus and drove off.

* * *

The Board of Education for Melbourne Public School System was located outside downtown Melbourne. It was a three-story building and had been on the corner of Valley and Seventh Street for thirty-seven years. The brick structure had an orange banner on the outside over the front door of the building that read *HAVEN OF SAFETY AND LEARNING,* in black bold letters.

Mora Abernathy's office, dedicated to special education for the cognitively disabled children, was located on the second floor.

Douglas arrived at eight-thirty a.m. Helene Dunbar, the receptionist, examined Douglas. She exhaled heavily before paging Mora.

Mora appeared seconds later and shook Douglas' hand.

"Mr. Pratt, thanks for being so prompt. My office is this way." Mora pointed down the hall.

Douglas nodded good morning and followed her down the hall to her office.

Mora had been Director of Special Education for the cognitively disabled children in the Melbourne Public School System for eleven years. Prior to this position she worked as a special education teacher in Blaine, Texas. Job searching on the internet led her to Melbourne.

Mora dated quite often. However, at thirty-eight, she still had not experienced a lasting relationship. She had a nicely curved figure and her short blonde hair gave her a Marilyn Monroe look.

Mora's sickenly sweet perfume overpowered the hallway. She swayed her hips excessively as she walked down the hall to her office. Douglas followed and pretended not to watch. Her lilac and white silk dress hugged her body, and was at least three inches above her knees. The round neckline and push up bra protruded her breasts upward and formed a gaping cleavage. Her calves bulged as she balanced herself on her four inch lilac pumps.

Helene shook her head and mumbled "bitch" as Mora walked down the hall. Douglas frowned at Helene, guessing these two women probably had differences.

Since his tenure with Melbourne Public School System, Douglas heard many rumors that Mora had the personality of a snake, she was vain and much into herself and her image of her impeccable beauty projected the self-belief that every man wanted her.

Mora's office was the last room on the left. Her office reeked of her floral perfume. The only picture on the wall was one of herself as she was embarking on an Alantis Cruise Ship. Plush tan carpet surrounded the floor.

"Have a seat, Mr. Pratt." Mora pointed to the chair across from her mahogany desk.

"You sounded like this is an emergency. What's the problem?" he asked.

Mora handed him the summons and complaint and sighed.

"Apparently, this Beverly Monday is filing charges against Melbourne Public School System. She's accusing one our teachers, Jennifer Reinhart, of abusing her retarded eight-year-old son, Bryce Monday."

As he read the complaint, Douglas thought that a trial was the last thing he wanted. Melbourne Public School System did not need any more negative publicity.

After he finished reading the charges he placed them on Mora's desk. "Are any of these allegations true?"

"I talked to Jennifer Reinhart and she claims not." Mora said. "When I interviewed Jennifer two years ago for the teaching position at Carter, she told me she was broke and in desperate need of a job. Jennifer, like myself, is a native of Texas, so out of compassion, I gave her the job at Carter Elementary. The position was the only opening at the time. I felt it couldn't be that difficult teaching severely handicapped children. There were only five children in the classroom, plus an aide. Jennifer needed a job and this was a good opportunity for her."

Confused, Douglas asked, "What do you mean, good opportunity for her?"

"She didn't have a car so this job was perfect for Jennifer. She told me she could walk to school because her apartment was only three blocks away. During the interview she also told me she was the youngest of two children, and her brother was a college professor at Blaine University in Texas. She was determined to prove to her parents she could make it. Jennifer's an unattractive woman and I felt sorry for her." Mora shrugged. "So sue me. No pun intended."

"Well, then we don't have a problem. They can't prove anything." Douglas smiled. "What about Robert Clayborn?"

Confident, Mora said, "Oh believe me, he will not cause a problem. I'm sure of it."

Douglas glanced over the charges again.

Mora stood, then walked around to the front of her desk. She perched atop the desk in front of Douglas, and crossed her legs at the knee. "May I call you Doug?"

Douglas never liked nicknames, but somehow he knew that even if he told Mora not to call him Doug, she'd do it anyway.

"Why is this woman suing Jennifer Reinhart, Robert Clayborn, the Melbourne Public School System and Boelter Insurance Company?" She asked.

"It's really quite simple. Jennifer Reinhart and Robert Clayborn don't have the kind of money that her attorney is probably going to ask for. The only way to collect is to go after the entire system and their insurance company. That's where the money is."

"There's a problem, Doug."

"Not really. They have to prove the abuse."

Mora slid from her perch and returned to her chair. "I wish it were that simple."

"What do you mean?" he asked.

"Doug, Jennifer Reinhart was never properly trained nor certified to teach handicapped children. I knew that when I hired her."

* * *

The early morning addition of the Melbourne Sentinel reported child abuse charges had been filed against the Melbourne Public School System. The article referred to the abuse of a cognitively disabled child as the most unspeakable crime of all.

Inez received phone calls from several reporters requesting interviews with her and her client.

Douglas contacted Jennifer Reinhart, Robert Clayborn and Mora Abernathy and instructed them not to answer any questions from the media.

CHAPTER NINE

Willie Flinn had not seen his son, Bryce, in seven years. When Bryce was born, he couldn't handle the fact that his child was cognitively disabled and would be that way for the rest of his life.

Beverly met Willie about eight years earlier at a block party. Seven weeks into the relationship, Beverly informed Willie she was pregnant. Willie was not the kind of man Beverly had imagined as the father of her children. He was sporadically employed and he loved hanging out in the streets. Beverly was rebounding from a previous relationship and wanted companionship. Getting pregnant was definitely not part of her plan.

Willie and Beverly started living together in her eighth month of pregnancy. Willie was lazy and domineering. When the doctor informed Beverly about Bryce's disability at birth, Willie blamed Beverly. He had two daughters from two previous relationships and they both were fine. He never let Beverly forget that.

Their relationship ended abruptly in a heated argument about money. Beverly never heard from Willie or his family.

When Beverly's phone rang, Willie was the last person she thought would be calling.

"Beverly, this is Willie. How's my son?"

"Bryce is fine. Why are you calling? What do you want?"

"Damn, can't a nigga call and check on his kid."

"Yes, except the nigger hasn't called in about seven years. You or your family."

"Girl, you always did have a sharp tongue. You cut a brother into pieces with your words."

"What do you want, Willie?"

"I heard what Bryce's teacher did to him. Is he okay?"

"How did you find out?"

"In the paper. I can read you know."

Beverly sighed and sat on the couch. "I'm having a hard time dealing with this shit."

"I haven't been much of a father to Bryce, but I want to be a part of his life."

Beverly knew Willie inside and out. She knew he wanted something. After seven years she seriously doubted he had a guilty conscience and suddenly wanted to be a good father.

Willie's priorities were screwed up. Willie never did anything unless there was something in it for him. Beverly knew he was definitely up to something. She decided to play along with him for as long as she could tolerate him.

"So tell me. How much cash are you and your fancy attorney suing for?" Willie asked. "I heard Inez Connors is a tough bitch in the courtroom."

Beverly was right. Willie hadn't changed.

"Why?" Beverly yelled. "Why do you want to know?"

"Listen, don't get smart with me. He's my son, too."

"Exactly what is it that you want, Willie?"

"I want to sue the sons-of-bitches for what they did to my son."

"You don't even care about your son. You see an opportunity to make some extra cash. That's all. You want to come back into Bryce's life and then when the trial is over, you'll disappear. I don't think so," she said.

Sounding angry, Willie said, "Bryce is my son, too, and I'm entitled to whatever he gets. I'm his father."

"You don't even care about what his teacher did to him, do you? He was physically abused over and over again. He screamed in pain because he could not speak. You want money for booze and drugs. You haven't changed and you probably never will. No, you can't file charges with me. I won't let you capitalize on my son's pain."

"Don't you get smart with me, Beverly. Remember if it comes out in court what you did, it could really hurt your case."

Surprised that Willie would even bring up the past, she said, "Bryce was only one year old. How dare you."

"How dare I? I'll tell you how dare I. You think you're going to get all the money for yourself. You're wrong. He's just as much my son as he is yours. If you don't do this, I'll tell what you did and you'll lose this case for sure."

Beverly slammed the phone down so hard she broke a nail.

* * *

Robert Clayborn called Mora around midnight after his family had gone to bed. "Mora," he whispered.

"What." She yawned.

"Look, I don't want any trouble."

"Relax Robert. Nothing's going to happen."

"I don't want my reputation damaged any more than it already has been. It'll ruin my marriage."

"Look, all you have to do is do exactly what I tell you to. Susan never has to know what happened. When we meet with Douglas Pratt next week, just tell him what I told you. Tell him that Ella Walker never came to see you. I want you to tell Mr. Pratt that all three, Ella Walker, Agnes Harris, and Galen Small, are lying because of their pending grievances against you."

"I don't like lying," Robert said.

"Don't piss me off. You picked a fine damn time to get scrupulous. Remember one thing, Susan is not the only one who'll be affected. Your career, not to mention mine, could go up in smoke. I've already fired Helene Dunbar because she refused to cooperate. She never liked me anyway, so she won't be missed."

"You fired the receptionist?"

"Look, I mean business, Robert. If you don't cooperate, fired is not the worst thing that will happen to you. Believe me, Robert, I'll ruin your professional and personal life."

CHAPTER TEN

After eight years, Beverly saw him for the first time at Inez's office. He was exactly the way she remembered him, muscular, six feet tall, and probably still weighed one hundred ninety pounds. His smooth, caramel-colored skin surrounded a perfectly trimmed mustache. His curly black hair highlighted his brown eyes. He had a blinding smile and a deep soothing voice that would capture the heart of any woman.

Beverly knew it was him when he called her name. She could never forget his voice and how it made her feel. Martin Townsend was Beverly's first true love. They were high school sweethearts.

Their relationship ended abruptly when Martin moved to Florida to care for his mother after his father died. His mother became quite ill and was too sick to travel. Martin transferred from Melbourne University to Florida State University to be near her.

Beverly attended Merrill College in Wisconsin. Beverly's relationship with Martin became long distance. They both mutually agreed it would remain that way until Martin's mother could travel. Martin and his mother would then return to Melbourne.

Four months later, Martin's mother died. Beverly flew to Florida for the funeral and stayed a week afterwards to help Martin with his mother's affairs.

With nothing holding him back, Martin still didn't return to Wisconsin. Instead, he asked Beverly to relocate to Florida. Martin had been offered a job with Dobbs and Smith Law Firm, the most prestigious firm in Florida. It was an offer that he couldn't refuse. Beverly graduated and landed a promising job with Bertram Group Insurance.

Their relationship was at a stalemate. After three months the weekend flights became too expensive and the phone calls were far and few. Neither one of them verbally ended the relationship, but contact diminished until it was non-existent.

Beverly agreed to meet Martin for dinner at Mama's Kitchen, one of their favorite restaurants.

When she arrived, Martin was already waiting for her and he waved her over to the table.

"I see you're still very prompt," Beverly said.

"Well some things never change." Martin pulled her chair out and she sat down.

"Yes, that's true." She smiled. "Some things never change, Mr. Townsend. You're still a gentlemen."

"And you're still gorgeous."

Beverly felt butterflies in her stomach and her knees weakened. "Thank you."

"When did you get back?" Beverly asked.

"Actually, I've been in Wisconsin for a year."

Beverly desperately wanted to ask him why in the hell hadn't he tried to contact her, but knew she couldn't. Maybe he was married or seeing someone and this dinner date was merely for old time's sake.

"What brought you back to Melbourne?"

"Inez Connors."

The waitress took their order. Beverly ordered smothered chicken with mashed potatoes and gravy. Martin ordered meatloaf. Beverly thought how ironic it was for her attorney and her ex-boyfriend to be lovers. In fact Beverly was beginning to get angry. Martin refused to move back after his mother died, but did for Inez.

When the waitress left, Beverly, as calmly as she could, asked, "You said Inez Connors is the reason you moved back?"

"Yes, I always kept up with the news in Wisconsin and when I read about her case involving the absentee landlord, I knew she had what I'd been looking for in a law partner, compassion for others. So I sent her my resume and you know the rest."

"What happened with your job at Dobbs and Smith?" She asked.

"They were good but I'm not in the habit of defending guilty people because they have megabucks. I don't operate like that and I never will."

Beverly sighed with relief.

"I know you so well, Beverly. After all these years you still can't hide when something's wrong. What's going on? Why were you seeing Inez? I saw a sadness in your face that day. It was the kind of look that you had when your grandmother died your junior year in high school. If it's too personal, I apologize. I don't mean to pry."

Beverly interrupted, "No. Nothing's personal when it comes to you. I found out that my son's teacher had been abusing him. I went to Inez and she filed a lawsuit against the school system."

"How old is your son?"

"Bryce is eight."

"He told you his teacher was hurting him?"

"He couldn't. You see, Martin, my son is cognitively disabled and couldn't tell."

Martin looked at Beverly, and she remembered her love for him.

He reached across the table and took her hand. "You and your husband must be devastated over this."

"What husband? Bryce's father and I were never married. We broke up when Bryce was about a year old."

"I'm sorry."

"Please don't be sorry. Willie couldn't handle Bryce's disability so he split. It was probably for the best because I would've eventually left if he hadn't, because of his drug and alcohol use."

Martin shook his head. "Bryce's disability shouldn't matter to him. He's his child. He should love him no matter what. He should want to be a part of his life even more because of his disability."

"I really don't want to talk about this anymore. I might start crying. Every time I think about how that woman hurt my baby, I get sick and angry enough to kill."

"I don't blame you. I would to." Martin cleared his throat. "Are you seeing anyone?"

Beverly quickly responded, "No, what about you? Any children?"

Martin smiled. "No, I'm not seeing anyone and I don't have any children.

Beverly returned a smile.

CHAPTER ELEVEN

When Inez's secretary informed her that Attorney Douglas Pratt was there to see her, she wasn't surprised. In fact, she expected him a few days ago when the school system first received notice of the lawsuit.

Douglas stroked his short blonde hair and sat in the royal blue, deeply contoured, executive high back, mahogany chair across from Inez's desk. He adjusted the chair to cradle his body and support his back. He crossed his legs carefully not to wrinkle the slacks of his brown Armani suit, twiddled his thumbs and stared at her. "Forgive me for not making an appointment, but I was in the neighborhood and I thought I would take a chance that you were in."

Inez clinched her lips to keep from laughing in his face. His office was located on the other side of town and he would never come into the neighborhood without a purpose. Inez wondered if the arrogant son-of-a-bitch sauntered into all of his opponents' offices and took a seat without asking. She doubted it. She, however, was prepared for his visit. She sat in her matching chair and stared back. She leaned over and confidently asked, "How much?"

"Excuse me." He uncrossed his legs and his brown eyebrows shot upward.

"How much is Melbourne Public School System willing to pay to settle out of court? That is why you're here, isn't it?"

"Look, I'm a busy man. I'll make this quick. Melbourne Public School System is prepared to offer your client fifteen thousand dollars to settle out of court, and the assurance that Jennifer Reinhart be relieved of her duties in the Melbourne Public School System. In fact, I'm told she's already been suspended pending the outcome of the investigation."

"Do you have children, Mr. Pratt? How would you feel if it were your child that had been abused?"

"My two sons attend Hillsboro, a private school in Ozaukee County."

Inez said, "Unfortunately, Mr. Pratt, not everyone can afford that luxury for their children." She wondered if Mr. Pratt had been a jackass all his life or did it happen with his union with Melbourne Public School System. She could not understand why Mr. Pratt didn't give a damn about what happened to an innocent child. She speculated how he was raising his sons, probably to act like they were better than everybody. Inez figured Mr. Pratt raised his children to only deal with kids on their same level.

"I read your complaint. Off the record, Ms. Connors, you can't win. Your client never took the child to the doctor. She never reported the alleged abuse to the police. The child certainly can't tell what happened. Fifteen thousand dollars is really a very generous offer for someone like Ms. Monday. I'm sure the child. . . ."

Inez interrupted, "Just what the hell do you mean, someone like Ms. Monday?" Inez hated to think that on top of his high-falutin' attitude, the bastard was prejudiced. Luckily for him it was off the record, or she'd bring his ass up on discrimination charges.

"I mean the child probably has many medical bills, and the money would definitely help. She's a single parent, probably with a limited income. Why waste the taxpayers' dollars on a long drawn out trial?"

Inez understood Mr. Pratt perfectly. Beverly was a black single woman, and stereotypically either on welfare or working a minimum wage job. No, he wasn't prejudiced, just an egotistical, self-serving son-of-a-bitch that probably didn't know any better.

Angry, but still in control, Inez said, "The taxpayers are paying this teacher's salary. She abused this child, and has no business teaching, and definitely shouldn't be around children."

"Allegedly abused," he corrected.

"The fact that you would even come here to make such a ridiculous offer is an insult to my client. Jennifer Reinhart will find another job teaching in another school system. But what about the next child? You know she did it, don't you? How do you live with yourself knowing that you are defending a guilty woman? What if she got a job teaching at Hillsboro? Tell me something, how much is Melbourne Public School System paying you? How much did they pay you for the out of court settlements you obtained on other cases involving disabled children in that school system?"

Inez exhaled and stared at Douglas. "How much did you get when the bus driver delivered a disabled child to the wrong address. The driver took off and never waited to see that the child made it inside. Luckily the woman who lived there wasn't a pervert and called the police. The child's mother went ballistic and publicly threatened to sue Melbourne Public School System for negligence. You settled out of court on that one." She smirked.

"Sounds like you've done your homework. Not bad for a female."

A male chauvinist pig too, Inez thought to herself. Douglas was really getting on her last nerve.

Furious, Inez stood, took one of her business cards from her desk and walked to the door. "I won't even dignify that chauvinistic remark with a comment. If you'll excuse me, I have work to do." Inez opened the door.

When Douglas reached Inez, he paused with his hand on the doorknob and shook his head.

"Mr. Pratt, I'd like your offer in writing. By law I have to notify my client of all offers no matter how ridiculous they may be."

Douglas glanced from the top of her head to her shoes, rolled his eyes and smirked. He started to leave.

"And Counselor," she added.

He exhaled, turned around. "What now?"

"Still off the record, don't be fooled by my gender. I eat jerks like you for breakfast." Inez handed Douglas her business card. "The next time you're in the neighborhood, call my office and make an appointment with my secretary. I'll see you in court." She slammed the door.

CHAPTER TWELVE

Inez attended her Mothers Against Drunk Drivers (MADD) meetings every Thursday evening at Savior Baptist Church from six-thirty until eight.

The Melbourne Chapter of MADD was founded in 1986 out of the heartbreaking death of a fifteen-year-old boy. The driver had previously been convicted three times of driving while under the influence of alcohol. The boy's mother was infuriated at the lenient laws for drunk drivers and focused her pain on trying to improve them. Since its existence, membership had grown to four hundred seventy-five.

Inez joined the Chapter to help with the fight to eliminate the crime of drunk driving and to find strength from the members to help her deal with the loss of her husband and child.

As a speaker for the group, Inez had addressed many high school and college students in the past ten months. The group crusaded through countless neighborhoods passing out red ribbons to be tied on car antennas as a constant reminder to not drink and drive.

Every time Inez took the podium to acknowledge a new member, she re-lived her horrible experience. The Chapter's newest member, Debra McCall was devastated a year ago when a drunk driver killed her ten-year-old son.

The six oblong stained glass windows on both sides of the room shined brightly as Inez walked to the front of the church.

Ms. McCall sat in the front row in the first seat. Inez gently squeezed the woman's shoulder as she stepped up to the podium. The back drop of the altar was a mural of Jesus Christ on the cross.

Inez swallowed hard, exhaled and studied Ms. McCall. "No one can know the pain and horror of losing a loved one to a drunk driver except those who have gone through it. Everyone in this room share in your grief and understand your frustration and anger. We've all been there. We struggle to get through each day and with the help of this group and God, we do. You are not alone. We have each other and together we will heal."

Inez smiled through tears and cleared her throat. Quiet filled the room as the members waited for Inez to continue.

"Ms. McCall, one evening eleven years ago, I received a phone call informing me to come to the emergency room at the hospital. When I asked why, I was told my husband and baby daughter had been in a car accident. When I arrived at the hospital, they both had been pronounced dead. I was told they were in a head-on collision with a drunk driver that swerved to the other side of the road. The driver who killed my family is a free man today."

Ms. McCall pulled a handkerchief from her purse and wiped her eyes.

Inez continued. "My life has never been the same since that day. I was angry at the world. I kept thinking why my husband and baby? Of all the people in the world, why my family? My little Allie was only nine months old. You always think of dying before your children. It seems unnatural for a parent to outlive a child. I thought no one could ever understand the hurt and pain I felt. I was wrong." Inez glanced around the room. "Everyone in this room understands."

Ms. McCall shook her head.

Inez wiped her tears. "I know you've probably asked yourself the same questions. Believe me, you did the right thing by coming to the meeting. I still have nightmares and I probably always will. Being a part of this group has helped me deal with my loss and make my life more productive. I refuse to allow my grief to consume me."

Ms. McCall walked up to the podium in tears and hugged Inez and spoke softly in her ear. "Thank you, Ms. Connors. Thank you for your kind words. God Bless you."

The members stood and applauded. Tears streamed down Inez's face.

CHAPTER THIRTEEN

Robert Clayborn left Mora Abernathy's office in a frenzy. The trial was only weeks away and each day he grew more nervous.

He couldn't sleep at night. He sensed his wife knew something was wrong, but he couldn't tell her. There was no way out for him. Mora had made that perfectly clear.

Robert tried to keep his personal problems in the past, but the trial would probably dredge them up. He loved his wife and son and the last thing he wanted was for them to find out what he had done. They would never forgive him.

He met Susan in college. They were both seniors and served on a committee formed to rally for better security. Non-students had robbed several students and this group wanted school officials to enlist the services of security guards and install lights in the student parking lot.

There were only ten in the group and they would meet to discuss ways and means of accomplishing their goals.

After about six months of pleading, protesting and picketing, and after a student was robbed at gun point, officials hired two security guards and installed lights throughout the parking lot.

The group celebrated their victory at a twenty-four hour café near the campus. They celebrated until around nine, then started to scatter.

Robert and Susan were the last ones to leave. They spent hours talking and sharing dreams and goals. They realized how much they liked each other and started dating. They dated five years and lost many friends during that time because of their friends' disapproval of interracial relationships.

He and Susan went through a lot to be together. Susan's family was adamant about her marrying a black man. Her parents made it perfectly clear to Robert that he was not what they had planned for their only child.

Susan was forced to make a choice, and she chose Robert Clayborn. Susan's parents didn't attend the wedding and their prejudices have prevented them from seeing their only grandchild.

Robert's family, in time, learned to tolerate their son's marriage to a white woman. After Eric was born, his parents visited. Robert's father would constantly say, "Boy, when she gets mad and calls you a nigger, then you'll know what I mean. White should marry white and black should marry black," he preached unsuccessfully to his son.

Susan remained strong in her commitment to her marriage throughout the years. If the truth came out, she would be devastated.

Robert started to drive home and wondered if, maybe, he should tell Susan the truth. If their love had survived through all the other obstacles, maybe, it would again. Robert knew he would be taking a chance if he told Susan. He knew he'd be risking everything. Could his marriage survive the truth? He thought not.

One thing he knew for sure was Mora meant every word she said. She was a self-righteous conniving little bitch and would do anything to get out of this mess, even expose his past.

All of a sudden Robert heard a horn blowing and tires screeching. He'd run a red light. He quickly slammed on the brakes and his car spun around.

The other driver, a young man probably in his middle twenties, in a red Jaguar, rolled down his window, waved his fist and yelled obscenities at Robert. "What the hell is your problem, old man? Didn't you see the motherfucking red light? You son-of-a-bitch, you could've killed me. Are you fucking blind?"

Robert gained his composure, then rolled down his window. "Oh my God. I am so sorry. Are you okay, son?"

Still outraged, the driver continued to yell vulgarities. "What the fuck are you doing? Hell no, I'm not okay. You almost killed me. Didn't you see the red light? You could've killed us both? Are you drunk? What the hell is your problem? You goddamn asshole."

Robert couldn't get a word in edgewise with this loud mouthed young man. He finally interrupted. "Look, nobody's hurt. That's the most important thing."

The driver continued to yell and scream at him. It was pointless trying to reason with him, so Robert rolled up his window and drove off.

He arrived home around six-fifteen that evening. His son, Eric, greeted him at the door. "Dad, what happened to you? Mom and I already finished dinner. We got tired of waiting." Eric continued before his father could respond. "I'm going to the playground to shoot hoops with some of the guys. I'll see you later. Oh Dad, mail's on the table." Eric dashed out the door.

Robert entered the living room and rested his briefcase on the glass cocktail table. He picked up the mail, sat on the royal blue sofa and paged through it. He glanced up at the fireplace. He walked over to the mantle and stared at his wedding photo. He looked at the portrait of Susan, Eric and himself that was mounted over the fireplace and sighed. He sat in the royal blue chair and kicked the white fringes on the blue, white and black oriental rug that was the focal point of the polished hardwood floor. Robert relaxed and was unaware of Susan's presence until she began to massage his shoulders. "Umm, that feels wonderful."

Susan came around the chair and sat in his lap. "I didn't know you were home. Why didn't you let me know?"

"I'm sorry, Dear." He wrapped his arms around her and kissed her on the lips. "I just got home."

"I expected you two hours ago. Why didn't you call me? I was worried."

Robert knew this was the opportune time to be honest with his wife. He could tell her about his meeting with Mora and hope she would understand. But instead, he chose to add another lie to his list of deceptions. "I was late because I had to attend a last minute school board meeting."

CHAPTER FOURTEEN

Jury selection was an all day process of interviewing a number of men and women from all walks of life. There were several reporters in the courtroom and a handful of spectators.

The Honorable Richard VanCulver was the presiding judge. Judge VanCulver had grown lazy over the years. Once six feet, lean and muscular, he was now a potbellied man whose partially pink bald head was covered with a salt-and-pepper toupee.

Judge VanCulver graduated from Dossimer High School in Wilmington, Delaware. He moved to Amherst, New Jersey where he studied law. He later moved to Wisconsin and attended Marquette University in Melbourne where he obtained his Bachelor of Science Degree in Law.

Beverly sat between Inez and her paralegal, Joey. Beverly helped take notes on each person during the jury selection process.

Somewhat familiar with this process, Beverly had been called for jury duty about three years ago. She was interviewed for a case in which a thirty-five year old male was to stand trial for allegedly molesting a five-year-old boy.

One of the questions asked by the defendant's attorney was if the prospective jurors had children and if so, their ages. Bryce was the same age as the victim and Beverly was disqualified for obvious reasons.

Jennifer Reinhart and Robert Clayborn sat at the defendant's table on the other side of the room with Douglas Pratt in the middle.

This was the first time Beverly had seen Jennifer since finding out about the abuse. Beverly stared at Jennifer from across the room. Not once did Jennifer look in Beverly's direction. Beverly felt angry and wanted desperately to approach Jennifer and ask her why she'd hurt Bryce. Beverly had a jittery feeling in her stomach and a weakness came over her body and filled her heart with sorrow.

The attorneys took turns asking a series of questions: "What is your full name?"

"Where do you live?"

"Where do you work?"

"What is your marital status?"

"Do you have children? If so, how many and how old?"

"Do you know any of the parties involved in this case?"

"How do you feel about handicapped children?"

"Do you know anyone who is handicapped or have a child who is handicapped?"

"Do you have any knowledge of this case?"

The morning was long and boring. Judge VanCulver started to doze off around eleven o'clock, then decided to recess for lunch. He rapped his gavel. "Due to the late morning hour I feel it would be appropriate if we break for lunch. This court is in recess until one o'clock this afternoon."

* * *

At Beverly's suggestion, Inez, Joey and Beverly had lunch at Mama's Kitchen, only a half block from the courthouse. Inez and Joey had never eaten in this establishment. Whenever Inez and Joey were in court, they always ate at House of Steaks across the street from Mama's Kitchen.

They sat in a window booth, Beverly sat across from Inez and Joey.

"Does this place serve steaks?" Joey asked.

"No," Beverly said, "but they have a meatloaf that's to die for. I think you'll really like it."

"This is my first time here. I'll try anything once." he said.

"You'll love it. Trust me," Beverly said.

Inez studied the menu. "I'm picky about soul food. I don't eat everybody's cooking. I see they have fried green tomatoes. I haven't had fried green tomatoes since the last time I went home."

Joey scanned the menu and looked at Inez. "I haven't had them since I was in law school. I can't believe that we've never considered Mama's Kitchen for lunch as much as we eat downtown."

"I know. Everything sounds delicious. Beverly, what do you suggest?" Inez asked.

"I think you both would love the meatloaf with the crowder peas and speckled butter beans, collard greens, fried corn, potato salad and cornbread."

"Stop." Joey raised his hand. "You're making me hungry."

Beverly looked down and twiddled her fingers. Her eyes darted around the room.

Inez asked, "Are you worried about the trial, Beverly?"

"Do you think you'll get justice for my son?"

"I'm going to do my best."

Joey reached over and patted Beverly's hand. "You must have faith and a positive attitude. Inez and I will do our best."

Beverly wiped the corner of her eye with her index finger. "Seeing Bryce's teacher for the first time since all this started was really hard. I look at her and I still have trouble believing what she did to Bryce. When Bryce hurt his lip, I believed her when she told me how it happened. I wonder now if she caused the bruise I saw on his back."

Inez and Joey looked at each other. Inez asked, "What bruise on Bryce's back?"

"I noticed a bruise on the lower part of Bryce's back a couple of months before school ended."

Joey asked, "Did you ask how he got it?"

"Did you take him to see a doctor?" Inez asked.

Beverly brushed the tears from her face. "I assumed he got the bruise from his book bag." She covered her mouth with her hand, muffled her voice and cried, "Oh my God."

Inez leaned forward. "Beverly, what's the matter?"

"I never took him to the doctor. I didn't question Jennifer Reinhart. I bought him another book bag."

Inez grabbed Beverly's hand. "Don't do this to yourself. It's not your fault."

Joey handed Beverly a napkin on the table. "Don't cry. She'll pay for what she did to your son and that's a promise. Don't blame yourself."

Beverly wiped her face with the napkin, sniffled and smiled. "I'm sorry. I didn't mean to start crying. Thank you both for being so compassionate."

The waitress came over to the table. "Is everybody ready to order?"

Beverly ordered the meatloaf, vegetables, cornbread and iced tea. Inez and Joey followed her lead.

"Inez, how long do you think it'll take before they finish with the jury selection?" Beverly asked.

"We should finish today. Trial could start as early as tomorrow," Inez replied.

Joey grinned. "Remember Judge VanWinkle is hearing the case. It could take longer."

"I thought his name was VanCulver." Beverly said.

Inez snickered. "It is VanCulver. He's sometimes referred to as Judge VanWinkle because he has a tendency to nod off in the courtroom."

Beverly frowned. "He seems old to still be a Judge."

Inez smiled. "I would guess he's probably in his middle sixties."

"In fact," Joey added, "I think it was in 1981 when the judge moved back to Wisconsin and started his own private law practice. I remember when he was elected Judge in 1987, he made it publicly known he planned to hold that position until he retired."

Inez looked at Beverly. "Don't concern yourself with the judge. The jury is the one who will decide Jennifer Reinhart's guilt or innocence. Twelve sympathetic jurors is what we need to bring Melbourne Public School System down."

The waitress delivered their food.

Joey sliced his meatloaf, stabbed a piece and tossed it in his mouth. "This is delicious. Inez, I think we got us a new place to eat."

Inez tasted her meatloaf. "Yes." She shook her head. "Definitely scrumptious."

Beverly smiled. "I'm glad you like it."

Beverly poked at her peas with her fork. "Jennifer Reinhart never even looked my way in court. Did you notice?"

Joey took a bite of his cornbread. "Yes. Neither did Robert Clayborn and Mora Abernathy."

Inez took a sip of her tea. "Undoubtedly per Pratt's instruction."

* * *

The afternoon process of jury selection ended around three o'clock. The jury consisted of eight women and four men. Of these twelve, ten were white, one black and one Mexican. They were:

Denise Thatcher, married, two children
Margaret Lewis, married, four children
Maxwell Cane, married, two children
Laurel Valentine, single, no children
Dominic Santiago, Mexican, divorced, one child
John Williams, single
Annie Mae Wallace, black, widow, four children
Brenda Booker, divorced, no children
Tianna Adams, single, one child
Erica Dankmeyer, single, two children
Ruth Beckom, married, one child
Louis DeChambre, the jury foreman, married, five children

All of them brought together because of a vicious act upon an innocent child.

* * *

Newspaper and television coverage of the case prompted Judge VanCulver to have the jurors placed apart from society. The publicity increased the possibility of the jury being swayed. The jurors would be sequestered at the Melbourne Inn, located one block from the courthouse.

Judge VanCulver announced that because of a conflict in his schedule, trial would begin at nine a.m. on September 30.

* * *

Inez had spent weeks preparing her case against Jennifer Reinhart, Melbourne Public School System, and Robert Clayborn. With only a few days left, she asked Joey to research the Wisconsin statutes regarding children with exceptional educational needs. This was a new area to her. She studied every area of exceptional education. She investigated policies and procedures of Melbourne Public School System in regards to cognitively disabled children. Inez's biggest problem was not having a medical report from a doctor to indicate that Bryce had been abused.

Joey's investigation revealed incriminating evidence against Melbourne Public School System.

Originally from Blaine, Texas, Jennifer received her teaching degree at the University of Laramee. When she graduated, she bounced from job to job until she was hired at Carter Elementary. Jennifer had a Bachelor's Degree in education. She never received her Master's Degree or any additional training in the area of special education, which was a requirement according to Wisconsin State Statutes.

Inez hoped the fact that Jennifer Reinhart was never qualified as a cognitively disabled teacher, along with the eyewitnesses, would outweigh the absence of medical evidence.

Inez knew Douglas Pratt was smooth and damn good at what he did. She had to be sure that no stone was left unturned. She spent countless hours with Ella Walker, Agnes Harris and Galen Small, going over their statements.

Mr. Pratt had hired Dr. Vaughn Guftason, behavior psychologist. At first Inez was nervous because of Dr. Guftason's impeccable reputation, but when he met Bryce, her worries were put to ease. The visit he had with Bryce and Beverly was not damaging in the least. Bryce did not display any negative behavior. Bryce didn't have any tantrums so Inez felt comfortable that Dr. Guftason's testimony would not damage her case.

Inez enlisted the services of Dr. Alice Thrasher, also a behavior psychologist.

Inez had a life-size doll made of Bryce to use in the courtroom for demonstration purposes. If the jurors could see what Jennifer Reinhart did to Bryce, it would have a greater impact on their verdict.

CHAPTER FIFTEEN

It didn't take long for Beverly and Martin to realize they had never stopped loving each other. Absence only made their hearts grow fonder.

Martin's first thought was to contact Beverly when he returned to Melbourne, but he assumed that being the wonderful woman she was, she was either married or in a serious relationship.

Eight years was a long time to be apart and Martin knew they had a lot to make up for. With the trial approaching, he wanted to do something for Beverly prior to the trial. Martin wanted Beverly to relax as much as she could because once the trial started, he knew she'd be tense.

When his last client left, a woman suing for divorce, he decided to surprise Beverly at work with a phone call.

"Martin, this is a surprise. You never call me at work. Something must be wrong. Is it?"

"No, on the contrary. Everything is fantastic."

Puzzled, Beverly asked, "Okay, then to what do I owe this phone call? You sound really happy."

"I am happy, but I'd be even happier if you'd say yes."

"Say yes to what?"

"Say you'll go away with me for the weekend?"

"Martin, I can't. Bryce starts a new school on Monday. The trial starts on the thirtieth. I couldn't possibly leave."

"Look, you seem so tense and you'll be even more tense when the trial starts. There's no telling how long the trial will last and I just thought you should at least try to unwind. I know you're a little nervous."

"Yeah, a little nervous is an understatement. I'm extremely on edge. I don't know how I'll be able to sit in the same room with

Bryce's teacher. It was hard enough during jury selection. I prayed for God to restrain me."

"Look Baby, the three of us, me you and Bryce, could go to Fantasy World. I think Bryce would love it. Besides I really want to get to know him."

"Bryce is with Sharon for the weekend. Whenever she's off on the weekends from the hospital she keeps Bryce. Let's do it after the trial."

"Well, why don't you and I go and we'll take Bryce next time. How's that?"

"Another time would really be better for me, Martin. Fantasy World is about a four hour drive and I've never been that far away from Bryce."

"You really are a safeguard when it comes to the little guy. I knew you'd be a protective parent. You're a really good mother. Bryce is so lucky to have you."

"Yeah," she sighed. "Where was my motherly instinct when his teacher was abusing him? How protective was I then?"

"Don't talk like that. You're a wonderful mother. You've got to be strong. How about I come and take you out to dinner this evening. Would you like that?"

"Mr. Townsend, you have a date."

* * *

Martin finished some paperwork then left the office around six o'clock. He saw Inez come out of the conference room. She was headed towards her office when Martin decided to follow her. "Inez. Do you have a minute?"

"Sure, Martin. Come in"

"I know your client."

"Which one?"

"Beverly Monday."

"Really. How?"

"I've known her since high school. We dated for years."

"Did she tell you about her case?"

"Yeah, she did. I hope you can help her. If there's anything I can do, please let me know."

"Sounds like you might be trying to rekindle something with Beverly." Inez smiled, "Pick up where you left off. Huh? She didn't even mention that she knew you."

"Beverly's a private woman. She's not one to discuss her personal business." Martin grinned. "I don't know if we can pick up where we left off, as you put it, but we're going to dinner tonight, taking it one day at a time. I'll see you later."

* * *

It was like old times with Martin and Beverly. They ate dinner at the Chalet on the Lake at eight o'clock. The view of the lake was romantic and the water sparkled in the moonlight. The plush rustic carpet along with the dim lights and soft music from the piano player enhanced an already perfect evening.

They found a booth in the corner, eyes fixed on each other like nothing and no one else existed or mattered.

Beverly wore a black satin dress. The delicate lace accentuated the v-neck bodice and was a romantic interpretation of the little black dress that she wore on her first date with Martin all those years ago. Her flowing short black hair framed her chestnut colored face.

"Martin, I'm glad you invited me to dinner."

"I wanted you to relax before the trial starts."

"I'm nervous about the trial. I don't understand why Inez wants me to testify. I didn't see anything."

"You're Bryce's mother and you can talk about his disability. I think the main reason is because Douglas Pratt will make it look like you're a single mother trying to make some money at someone else's expense."

Beverly's voice started to tremble with anger. "Trying to make some money? Single mother? I've been on my job for probably longer than he's been practicing law. I don't think $75,000 a year would qualify me as destitute."

The waitress arrived at their table. "Hello, my name is Sara." She placed two menus on the table. "I'm your waitress this evening. I'll be back shortly to take your order."

Martin reached across the table and patted Beverly's hand.

"I said I wanted you to relax and that's what you're going to do. No more talk about the trial. We have a lot of catching up to do."

"But. . . ."

Martin interrupted, "No buts."

Martin picked up the menu. "What do you have a taste for?"

"I'm not sure." Beverly picked up the menu. "I can't decide between the steak and baked pork chops."

"Beverly, remember what we used to do when you couldn't decide?"

"What?" Beverly smiled.

"You'd order one and I'd order the other, then we would share."

"I remember." She laughed.

The waitress returned. Beverly ordered pork chops and Martin ordered steak.

"Martin, would you excuse me for a minute. I'm going to call Sharon. I want to check on Bryce."

The waitress came back to the table.

"Sir, I'm sorry, would you and your wife like something from the bar?"

Martin smiled at the waitress. He wasn't going to tell her Beverly was not his wife. If that was the assumption she made, then so be it. He wondered if others in the restaurant thought the same thing. "Yes, as a matter of fact you can bring us both a glass of your best white wine."

Beverly returned to the table.

"How's Bryce?"

"He's sleeping. Sharon's going to drop him off in the morning. I think she gets upset when I call to check on Bryce. She's always telling me I worry too much."

"He'll be just fine. By the way, how is your sister?"

"Sharon's fine. She's married to a really nice man."

"How's your mother?"

"Martin, my mother died last October."

Martin's eyebrows shot upward and his body sprung forward. "What?"

"Yes, she died. The doctors diagnosed her as having bone cancer a year prior to her death."

"Why didn't you call me? I would've been there. You were there for me when my mother died."

"We hadn't talked in years. How was I to find you? You never bothered to call me to let me know you had moved back to Melbourne, remember?"

Martin shook his head. "I'm so sorry."

The waitress returned with their drinks.

Beverly smiled. "You said we are going to have fun and not talk about sad things. So let's do that. No more talk about the trial or my mother." Beverly lifted her glass.

"Beverly, you haven't changed. You're still the same caring and considerate person you were in school." Martin met her glass in the air and they toasted before sipping the wine.

Beverly beamed. "You haven't changed either."

The waitress returned to the table with their dinner. Beverly gave Martin a pork chop and he cut his steak in half and shared with her.

* * *

After dinner they went to Rhythm Oasis to listen to music. It was oldies but goodies night and they heard many of the songs from their high school days.

The club was crowded. They stood in a corner with their glass of wine and listened to the music. A couple at the bar left and they quickly made their way over to the unoccupied seats.

"Wow, Beverly, I haven't heard these songs in ages. Let's dance."

They danced to several songs. At eleven o'clock, people started to leave, allowing for more room to maneuver. Martin and Beverly moved to a table for two near the dance floor.

Martin examined the room and noticed two women wearing the same outfit. "Beverly, remember when we went to prom and three girls wore the same dress as yours?"

Beverly laughed. "I'll never forget it. It wasn't funny back then. I was so mad. I wanted to be totally different from everyone. I spent weeks shopping for my dress. I just knew my dress would be different from the rest."

"Whatever happened to Roger Allen and Margaret?" Martin snapped his finger. "I can't remember Margaret's last name."

"Scott was her last name and they got married."

Martin sipped his wine. "I'm not surprised. Everybody said they would."

"Everybody also said the same thing about us, huh?" Beverly said before thinking. She didn't want to talk about what could have been. She didn't want to upset Martin. She was having a wonderful time and she sure as hell didn't want to spoil it with her insensitivity. "I'm sorry Martin. I didn't mean that."

"You meant it. You probably didn't mean to say it, but you meant what you said."

Martin extended his hand to Beverly. "Let's dance."

She took his hand and he escorted her to the dance floor. They danced to Natural High, one of their favorite songs in high school.

* * *

Martin and Beverly left Rhythm Oasis around twelve-thirty. Martin took Beverly home.

"Martin, I had a nice evening. It was relaxing and enjoyable. It was because of the company. Thank you."

Beverly unlocked the door and Martin followed her into the living room.

"I want to see you again." Martin said.

Beverly walked over to the couch and sat. "I have a son with a disability. The trial is coming up."

Martin sat beside her. "I know all that and I don't care. Bryce is a child. That's all I see. He's a part of you and how could I not want him. I've rearranged my appointments. I'll be at the trial with you every day until it's over. I'm doing this because I care."

"Martin, there are things you don't know. I have to tell you about Willie."

Martin put his index finger on Beverly's lips. "Sh-sh, I don't care about Willie. I don't want to know. All I know is when I saw you after all these years I realized why I could never find happiness in other relationships. I could never truly commit to a woman. You and I have unfinished business and I think we should give each other a chance. We never finished what we started years ago."

"Martin, things aren't the same. We're both different. We just can't pick up where we left off."

Martin grinned. "Let's start and see where we end up."

Martin wrapped his arms around Beverly and held her tightly. She embraced him around his waist. He held her face in his hands and softly pressed his lips against hers. He smothered her face with kisses.

Beverly returned his affection. "Oh Martin, I want that so much."

Martin held her tighter and caressed the back of her neck. "I promise we'll never be separated again."

CHAPTER SIXTEEN

Inez taught Sunday school to pre-teens, ages ten to twelve, at the Church of the Triune God from eight-thirty a.m. until nine-fifteen.

She had been so busy preparing for trial, she had not given much thought to Sunday's lesson. Inez decided to let the young adults pick the topic for discussion.

The group met in the basement of the church in the daycare classroom. There were seven in her group, five girls and two boys.

The children wanted Inez to tell them the story of Adam and Eve. That was their favorite and one that Inez had told many times. For forty-five minutes the children sat and gave Inez their undivided attention.

Church service started at ten o'clock. During the prayers for the sick and shut-ins, Reverend James Bonner surprised Inez and extended a special prayer for her. He prayed for the Lord to grant her the strength to find justice for Bryce.

Service lasted an hour. Inez overheard two of the members talking about the trial afterwards. Inez was glad people still remembered and hopefully there would be a roomful of spectators in the courtroom to support her case.

Inez arrived home from church around eleven-thirty and called her parents. "Hi Mom."

"Inez, Honey, how are you?"

"I'm fine. How are you and Dad?"

"Oh we're just fine. Dad's on the extension."

"How's my little girl?"

"Dad, I'm not a little girl."

"We've gone through this before. You'll always be my little girl. I don't care how old you are."

Inez smiled. "I know, Dad."

"What have you been up to?" Her mother asked.

"I have this case. It's a really sad one. I can't tell you the details, but it's about a handicapped little boy who was abused by his teacher."

Her mother sighed. "My goodness. How could anyone harm a child? What is this God forsaken world coming to?"

"I ask myself that over and over. I don't understand. I know one thing, I have to get a conviction. Not just for that child, but for all children who could end up in the same situation."

"Dad and I know you'll do well. We have faith in you and you must have faith and believe too."

"I do. I guess I just needed to hear you tell me. I'm going to be busy with the trial. So don't worry if you don't hear from me."

"Take care, Honey and keep in touch." Dad added.

"I love you, Mom and Dad. I'll talk to you soon."

Inez called Joey and they met at the office that afternoon at two o'clock and prepared for trial.

* * *

Sharon took Bryce home around ten o'clock the next morning and was surprised when Martin opened the door wearing only his slacks. "Martin, how are you?"

"I'm fine, Sharon. How have you been?"

"Really good. Thanks." Sharon looked around him. "Where's Bev?"

"She's still asleep." He knelt and lifted Bryce in his arms. "I'll take him and we'll hang out until Beverly wakes up." Martin kissed Bryce on the forehead. "How about I make us some pancakes."

Bryce cooed. Sharon smiled, stroked and kissed the back of Bryce's head. "I'll see you tomorrow, sweetie."

Martin sat on the couch with Bryce on his lap. He removed Bryce's jacket. "Did you have fun at Auntie Sharon's?"

Bryce started to drool. Martin grabbed a tissue from the box on the glass silver trimmed cocktail table. "Let me wipe your mouth, pal."

Bryce jerked and began to kick.

Martin held him tighter and rubbed his hair. "It's okay Bryce. What's the matter? I just wanted to wipe your mouth."

Bryce stopped kicking and put his head on Martin's chest.

Martin kissed him on top of his head. "How could anybody not want you? Your father must be an absolute idiot for not being a part of your life. You have me now. I'd say that makes me a lucky guy."

Wearing a white satin robe, Beverly entered the room. "I'd say that makes my son and me lucky."

"I didn't realize you were awake. How long have you been standing there?"

"Long enough to hear the nice things you said to Bryce." She walked over, sat next to Martin and kissed him on the lips. "Good Morning."

"I was just telling Bryce I was going to make us breakfast."

Beverly took Bryce from Martin and hugged him. "How's my little guy this morning?"

Bryce stared.

Martin looked at the tissue in his hand. "Bryce was drooling and when I wiped his mouth, he freaked out. Has he ever done that before?"

"Yes, but he never used to. I don't know why. Maybe, he doesn't like the texture of the tissue. I've been putting the tissue in his hand, guiding him to wipe his own mouth. He seems to tolerate that better."

Martin stood, took Bryce from Beverly. "I'll have to remember that."

Bryce rested his head on Martin's shoulder. Martin headed toward the kitchen. "I'm hungry, how about you?"

CHAPTER SEVENTEEN

Sharon and Beverly always shopped for Bryce's back-to-school clothes together. Sharon felt left out when Beverly called and informed her she and Martin would be taking Bryce shopping.

She was a bit jealous since Martin and Beverly had rekindled their relationship. Sharon kept Bryce during the summer, but now she had to share him with Martin. Martin would pick Bryce up from Sharon's and if he didn't have any early morning appointments, he would keep Bryce and drop him off at Sharon's later in the day.

Sharon was happy Beverly and Martin had found each other, but her time with Bryce and her sister suffered in the process.

She decided to invite Beverly, Martin and Bryce to dinner on Friday night. It would be a wonderful opportunity for Sharon to spend some quality time with her sister and nephew.

Beverly, Martin and Bryce arrived around six-thirty. Martin met Tyler for the first time. Tyler invited Martin to a game of pool in the recreation room downstairs, while Sharon and Beverly finished preparing dinner.

Martin took Bryce by the hand. "You come with me pal and I promise not to beat your uncle too bad at pool."

Sharon and Beverly went to the kitchen.

"You sit, Beverly," Sharon said. "I didn't invite you to dinner to put you to work."

"You're going to need help cutting that corn off the cob, so just bring the bag of ears to the table, give me a knife and let's get started. Besides, I know you remembered that fried corn is Martin's favorite. That's why we're having it."

Sharon brought corn and a bowl to the table, got a knife from the drawer and gave it to Beverly. She sat at the table. "Okay, if you say so."

They both started husking the corn and slicing the kernels from the cob into the bowl.

Sharon wanted to talk to Beverly about her relationship with Martin, but she didn't want to be the one to bring it up. She kept glancing at Beverly, hoping she would.

"You know, Sharon, it's been a long time since I've had fried corn," Beverly said.

Finally, Sharon couldn't wait. "You and Martin look happy together. Just like you did years ago."

Beverly stopped cutting corn. "I'm happy. Martin loves Bryce and in spite of the trial hanging over my head, I guess I'm happy too."

"I can see it. I'm a bit jealous."

"Why? Tyler is wonderful."

"No, I don't mean like that. I don't see you and Bryce as much. I used to keep him all day when school was out. That's why I switched to third shift at the hospital because I know you didn't want to leave him at a day care. Martin drops him off late and picks him up early which takes away my time with him."

"Sharon, Bryce loves you. He can't tell you, but he does. No one can ever change that. It goes without saying how I feel about you."

"Girl, I know. I'm being silly. I'm happy for you. Martin still looks good. He hasn't changed a bit."

"He's still the best thing that ever crossed my path. This time, we're going to stay together. I really think so."

"What brought him back to Melbourne?" Sharon asked.

"Would you believe that he's Inez Connor's law partner. I saw him when I met with Inez about the abuse."

"It's fate, Beverly. Fate brought you to Inez which led you to Martin."

"At first I was upset because he's been back in Melbourne for over a year and never even bothered to call me." Beverly grabbed another ear of corn.

"Did he have an explanation?" Sharon asked.

"Martin said he assumed I was with someone and he didn't want to disrupt my life. Boy, was he wrong."

"I haven't seen you this happy in a long time. Some things are just meant to be and I think you and Martin are one of them."

"He's rearranged his appointments so he'll be able to come to the trial every day."

Sharon smiled. "You know Mama always liked Martin. She would be so happy that you and Martin are together again. She sure as hell didn't like Willie. Speaking of Willie, when's the last time you heard from that loser?"

Beverly thought about Willie's blackmail attempt and how he could ruin her case if he were to follow through with his threats. Willie had not tried to contact her since the phone call, so his intimidation must have been frivolous. She decided not to tell Sharon. "It's been awhile since I've heard from Willie. Trust me, Sharon, I know Willie's history. He's probably somewhere so high or drunk he doesn't even know what day of the week it is. To tell you the truth, I hope he stays that way."

"He is Bryce's father."

Beverly shrugged. "I don't give a shit if he is." Agitated, she began to vigorously slice the kernels off the cob. "He's gone and I hope he stays gone."

"Okay, Beverly, I didn't mean to upset you. Let's finish so we can eat."

"I'm sorry, I didn't mean to snap at you. If Willie came back into my life, it could cause problems between Martin and me."

Sharon stopped slicing kernels and placed her hand on her sister's knee. "Let's not even mention his name. You know Mama used to always say if you don't want to be bothered with somebody, don't talk about them, otherwise you'll dredge them up." She smiled.

* * *

Martin and Tyler were on their third game of pool, the tiebreaker. Tyler twitched his mustache as he meticulously aimed the pool stick at the center of the white ball, staring at the five ball. "Five ball in the side pocket."

Martin sat in the chair with Bryce on his lap. He stroked Bryce's hair as he waited for his turn. "One of these days, I'm going to teach you how to play pool."

Bryce made incomprehensible sounds.

"Your turn, Martin. Nothing left but the eight ball for both of us. This will tell all."

Martin stood and put Bryce back in the chair. "You sit here now. This will only take a minute and then we can go upstairs and eat."

Martin rubbed his curly black hair, grabbed his pool stick from the corner. He took a piece of chalk that rested on the corner of the table and rubbed it at the end of his stick. He blew the powder from the tip of his pool stick, walked around to the long side of the rectangle pool table, bent slightly and aimed. "Eight ball in the side pocket," he said. He jabbed the white ball with his stick, forcing it into the eight ball, knocking the eight ball in the side pocket.

"Tyler, my brother," Martin smiled, "I hope I didn't beat you too badly in front of your nephew."

Tyler grinned. "Not at all. In fact I was just being hospitable. You know, since this is the first time I met you, and since this is my home, I felt the right thing to do was to let you win."

Tyler extended his hand. "Rematch brother?"

"You got it. Just let me know when." They shook hands.

Tyler lifted Bryce from the chair. "How about we go upstairs and check on dinner. I'm starved."

Bryce grinned and extended his arms to Martin.

"Martin, I think he wants you to take him." Tyler said.

Martin reached for Bryce. "Yeah, this little guy and I have become close. Right Bryce?" Martin hugged him. Bryce rubbed his cheeks and cooed.

"Sharon told me you and Beverly go way back?"

"We dated in high school. Circumstances separated us."

"Bryce sure likes you."

"I love him."

"Beverly's really going to need your support with the trial coming up."

"And she's got it. I care about her and nothing and no one will ever separate us again."

"I heard that my brother."

They slapped five.

"Let's check on dinner. I'm starved." Tyler said.

CHAPTER EIGHTEEN

Fall was Beverly's favorite time of the year, but she dreaded it too, because it was back to school for Bryce.

Although Bryce would be attending Palmer Elementary School, it was still part of Melbourne Public School System and her fear for his safety was of grave concern to her.

The cool breeze and the blanket of yellow and orange leaves covering the lawn was indicative that summer was gone.

It was seven forty-five a.m. School had started and she knew she'd better hurry. Holding Bryce's hand, she stood in front of the wide, city block long concrete building. As they started up the stairs, she noticed the orange banner over the front door of the school, *HAVEN OF SAFETY AND LEARNING*, in bold black letters. She remembered this banner over the front doors of Carter Elementary. She looked around the outside of the building, shook her head and swallowed hard.

Beverly noticed the fenced-in playground and the street crossing guard at each corner of the school.

She held Bryce's hand tighter, dropped her head and prayed out loud. "Oh God, please watch over my baby. I put his safety in your hands. Protect him and keep him out of harm's way, Amen!"

Beverly looked at the card she had received in the mail two weeks before the start of school that gave Bryce's room number. She felt an ominous sense of opening the door to a prison where she planned to deposit her son, as she opened the barred and screened green steel door and stepped inside.

She glanced down the corridor and the smell of freshly painted walls overwhelmed her. The floors shined with wax. She saw a handful of kids scattered about, hurrying to their classrooms because the bell had started to ring.

Beverly and Bryce started up the flight of stairs. Bryce's room was the first room located at the top of the third floor, number three hundred. They climbed the stairs slowly. She was in no hurry to get there.

When they reached their floor, she hesitated for a moment, then knocked on the door. A tall, medium build black man with a full gray beard came to the door.

"Hello, come in. My name is Patterson Drake." He leaned down. "You must be Bryce Monday."

Beverly held Bryce's hand tighter and stepped inside. "How do you know who he is?"

"I've only four students this year, and three have already arrived."

Still holding Bryce's hand, Beverly gazed around the room at the numbers and alphabets covering the walls. The other three children, one boy who appeared to have Down's Syndrome and two girls, one whose head was unusually large and the other girl rocked back and forth and occasionally burst into loud laughter, sat at a wooden round table in back of the room. A white man who was totally bald and beady-eyed sat at the table with the children. The children wore their book bags and were noisy as the bald man attempted to remove them.

Mr. Drake gently grasped Bryce's other hand, which startled Beverly.

"What are you doing?" Beverly pulled Bryce closer to her.

"I was going to take Bryce to his chair with the other children and introduce him to Ed Trundle, the Handicapped Children's Assistant."

Beverly started towards the table. "I'll take him." She took Bryce to the table, removed his book bag and sat him in the chair.

Mr. Trundle extended his hand. "Hi, I'm Ed Trundle. I'll be working with your son."

Beverly shook his hand. "I'm Beverly Monday and this is Bryce."

Mr. Trundle extended his hand and Bryce just stared into space.

"Mr. Trundle, I need to have a word with Mr. Drake."

"Sure, go ahead." Mr. Trundle put his arm around Bryce. "We'll be right here." Bryce gazed into space.

Beverly stroked Bryce's hair before walking over to Mr. Drake's desk. "I need to talk to you about something."

"Surely, what is it?" Mr. Drake asked.

She glanced at Bryce while addressing Mr. Drake. "First of all, my son doesn't like milk in a cup."

She stared at the floor and wondered if Mr. Drake was familiar with the lawsuit. Beverly peeked at Bryce again. Mr. Trundle was trying to teach Bryce how to shake hands. The other children stood, extending their hands to Bryce, emulating Mr. Trundle. Bryce stared at them all.

"Mr. Drake, I'll be blunt. My son was physically abused by his teacher at Carter Elementary. The teacher was not trained to teach disabled children, had never been certified."

"I understand your concern." Mr. Drake offered her the chair at his desk.

Beverly examined the classroom. "I look at this room and it's almost a replica of his classroom at Carter. All I can think about is the pain my son endured. The phone on the wall," she pointed, "is to immediately handle emergencies. Why didn't someone use the phone when Bryce needed help?"

"Ms. Monday, I can assure you nothing like that will happen here. All of the décor in the exceptional education classrooms in Melbourne Public School System are basically the same."

Beverly wondered if Mr. Drake was a child molester. Maybe, he and Mr. Trundle were sicker than Jennifer Reinhart and took turns with the kids. After all, these children can't tell about what happens to them. Beverly was scared. Maybe, they would be okay, not because they were on the straight and narrow, but because they knew she'd be watching.

God wouldn't let this happen twice to her son. She was sure the school system's employees was aware of the charges. They'd be careful with Bryce. They'd be afraid not to. "I know my son can be trying at times. I know better than anybody, but there is never reason enough to justify hurting any child. Mr. Drake, if ever you feel like you can't handle him, like it's just too much for you to deal with, please call me. I'll drop whatever I'm doing and come get him. If you tell me you can't handle him, no hard feelings, I'll come for him."

Beverly pleaded. "Whatever you do, please don't touch him." She wiped her eyes with the sleeve of her coat.

Mr. Drake nodded and patted her shoulder.

CHAPTER NINETEEN

It was September 29, Inez's daughter, Allie's, birthday and also one day before the trial. Inez bought six pink and six yellow roses to place on her daughter's grave. She bought a dozen red roses to place on her husband, Allen's, grave, which was next to Allie's.

It was a cool sixty-two degrees. The trees were bare and the grass had started to turn brown. Fall was a sad season for Inez. Her family was killed during the fall eleven years ago. Watching everything die around her was depressing. She often wondered why people couldn't come back to life in spring like the grass and the trees. Death might be easier to deal with.

Allie would be twelve today. How would she look now? What foods would she like? What would her favorite color be? How would she be doing in school? Would she get all A's on her report card? What would she want to be when she grew up? Would Inez have had more children and how would the siblings interact? What kind of voice would Allie have? Would she be easygoing or assertive? Inez would never know. All this was taken away when her daughter's life ended at the hands of a drunk driver.

She placed the roses on Allie's grave and sat with her head down. She stroked the teddy bear inscribed on the memorial stone. After a few minutes she started to cry and put her head against Allie's cold pink marble headstone. "My sweet baby. Mommy loves you and I miss you so much. Happy birthday baby." She wept out loud.

Inez wiped her tears and peered at Allen's grave. She laid the red roses in front of his pale blue stone marker. "My darling, I miss you, too. I have this case and I know you would be proud to be a part of it. I feel so incomplete without you. I'll always love you.

Take care of our little girl and give her a kiss for me." She stood and prayed in silence, before returning to her car.

Inez hated being alone on this day, so she decided to visit Joey.

Joey was a quiet man. He had worked with Inez on numerous cases. He was her right hand man. Joey was directly responsible for Inez's victory against the slum landlord. His investigation and diligence proved to be an asset to Inez.

Joey never wanted to be an attorney. He liked staying in the background. Investigating and exploring the law was his forte. Joey could design a case that would make F. Lee Bailey take note. He enjoyed watching Inez in action. The way she recited the intricate components of the law so that any laymen would understand was amazing, and knowing he contributed gave Joey great pride.

Joey's desire not to be in the forefront caused the demise of a four-year relationship with Sheila. Sheila didn't want a man in the background. Sheila felt black men had been in the background long enough and when Joey expressed his desires, Sheila slapped him with an ultimatum. Joey chose his career choice, not Sheila's choice.

Joey was reading over the teachers' statements when Inez rang the doorbell.

"Inez. This is a surprise. Come in."

She entered and started to pace.

"I know that walk. What's wrong? Are you nervous about the trial tomorrow?"

She stopped, turned and looked at Joey. "Just a bit depressed. Today's Allie's birthday and I went to the cemetery to put flowers on her and Allen's graves." She exhaled heavily. "Today is just not a good day."

"I understand. Sit down. You need a drink."

Joey went to the kitchen. Inez threw her hands up in the air in disgust.

"I don't need a damn drink. A drink is why my life is so fucked up. The son-of-a-bitch had too many drinks. That's why my life is shit. Don't you know that drinking is what killed my husband and baby? Drinking is the reason why I don't have my family."

She swallowed hard to catch her breath. She sat on the white leather couch, removed a handkerchief from her purse and wiped her teary eyes.

"Inez," Joey said. "Look at me. What do I have in my hands?"

Inez looked up at Joey and saw a bottle of flavored water in his right hand and two glasses of ice in his left. She sighed. "Joey, I'm so sorry. I know you would never offer me liquor."

He walked over, gave her a glass of ice and poured her some water. He poured some for himself and sat next to her. "Don't worry about it. I know you're upset. I really believe that all things happen for a reason. I think God took your baby and husband because he had something special planned for them. You just have to have faith and believe they're in good hands."

"I know, but it's hard sometimes. Especially today because it's her birthday."

"Inez, you'll find happiness with someone else. One day, you'll have more children. You have to give yourself a chance to love and to be loved. I think your husband would want you to find happiness with someone else. He wouldn't want you to wallow in self-pity."

"It's not going to happen anytime soon, but I thank you for the pep talk. I feel much better now."

Inez noticed the teachers' statements and other papers on the glass cocktail table. She picked up Ella Walker's statement. "You're working on the case, huh?"

"Yeah, just going over some last minute details. I don't foresee any problems. Jennifer Reinhart was not qualified to teach handicapped children. She should have never been in that type of classroom in the first place."

"Joey, remember who the attorney is. Douglas Pratt is sharp and cunning. He's got something up his sleeve. He always does."

Joey took a large swig of water. "What could it possibly be? We have three eyewitnesses. Jennifer was never qualified. How can a jury not find her and the system guilty?" He shrugged. "I mean so what if Beverly Monday didn't take Bryce to the doctor when she saw the bruise on his back. Pratt could refute that, but not an eyewitness to the abuse." Joey chuckled. "And Ella Walker is ready to tell what happened."

Inez sipped her water. "Mr. Pratt came to see me shortly after charges were filed. He offered an out of court settlement of fifteen thousand dollars."

"Why such a small amount?" Joey asked.

"He probably thinks Beverly is a welfare recipient and in need of money and would jump at an offer like fifteen thousand dollars. Even still, Joey, when I informed him my client refused, wouldn't you think he'd counter offer with a higher amount?"

"Not necessarily. I think he's bluffing. He's going to say these teachers are retaliating against Robert Clayborn because of previous problems. Even if that were true, what about Jennifer Reinhart? Pratt could say Mrs. Walker is retaliating against the teacher because of other problems in the classroom, but not Galen Small and Agnes Harris."

Inez nodded. "You got a point there."

Joey said, "We've got a behavior psychologist with impeccable credentials. We'll be ready for whatever Douglas Pratt has in store."

Inez smiled. "I'm glad I got you on my side."

Joey smiled and they toasted each other.

* * *

Douglas met briefly with his clients to go over the case. Everything was in order. He spent the evening preparing his opening statement to the jury.

* * *

Beverly put Bryce to bed around eight-thirty p.m. She went to her room and kneeled at her bedside and prayed out loud. "Dear Lord, tomorrow is the trial. I know that you will make sure justice is served. Watch over my child and all my loved ones. Please grant

Inez Connors the strength to tell Bryce's story. She'll be the voice that he doesn't have and it is through her that he will speak."

Beverly started to cry profusely. Still on her knees she sat back on the heels of her feet and held her stomach. "Forgive me, Lord, for not knowing what was going on in the classroom. I should have been a better mother. I should have been more protective of Bryce. I failed my son because I should have been more sensitive. I was blinded by Jennifer Reinhart's kindness and my blindness hurt my son. I was naïve and this caused my child harm. I promise I'll be a better mother, God. I'll never let harm come to Bryce again. You're a merciful God and I beg your forgiveness—Amen!"

CHAPTER TWENTY

It was September 30, the first day of the trial. Everyone gathered in the courtroom. The crowd was not what Inez had expected. The courtroom was about half full and as far as she could tell, only one reporter.

Douglas arrived thirty minutes early. He stood and greeted Inez as she walked in the courtroom with Joey at her side. "Good Morning, Counselor."

Inez nodded. "Mr. Pratt."

Douglas nodded at Joey and he responded with a nod.

Inez placed her briefcase on the plaintiff's table and exited the courtroom. Joey started to organize papers and the questions he and Inez had prepared for the witnesses.

Moments later Inez returned to the courtroom with Beverly. Beverly sat at the plaintiff's table between Inez and Joey. Beverly looked over at the defendant's table. Jennifer Reinhart and Robert Clayborn sat at the table with Douglas Pratt in the middle. Mora Abernathy represented Melbourne Public School System. She sat directly behind Douglas, the second seat in from the aisle, in the second row. Mr. Clayborn's wife, Susan, sat next to Mora in the first seat.

Police Officers Carl Edwards, short and stocky, and Neil Olson, red-headed and lean, stood on either side of the front of the courtroom.

Inez patted Beverly on the shoulder. "Are you okay?"

"Yes, I'll be fine. I hope Bryce is okay in the hallway with Sharon."

"He'll be just fine. Don't worry. She won't have to be here long with Bryce. I'll make sure of that," Inez said.

Ella Walker entered the courtroom and sat behind Joey.

A hand landed on Beverly's shoulder from behind. She turned around. "Martin, you made it."

Martin revealed his pearly whites and winked. "I told you I'd be here. I was held up in traffic."

Ella tapped Beverly on the shoulder. "Remember me?"

"Of course, I remember you, Mrs. Walker."

"Ms. Monday, I want you to know I tried to protect Bryce."

Beverly wanted desperately to ask Ella why she didn't say something sooner about what was going on in the classroom. How could she let it go on for so long? She decided it was best to let Inez handle it. "Thanks for coming forward, Mrs. Walker." She turned toward the front.

It was about nine-ten a.m. when the bailiff, Mr. Evans, called out, "All rise, court is now in session. The Honorable Richard VanCulver presiding."

Mr. Evans was a petite, spry old man. His wrinkled skin indicated that he probably could have retired awhile ago.

Judge VanCulver entered the courtroom wearing his black robe. He immersed his fleshy body in his brown high back swivel chair. He rubbed the patches of salt and pepper hair on either side of his temples, removed his glasses and asked, "Any business from either counselor before I bring the jury in?"

"None, Your Honor," Inez said.

"None, Your Honor," Douglas reiterated.

Judge VanCulver signaled and Mr. Evans slowly exited the courtroom. After a few minutes, Mr. Evans returned with the twelve jurors.

The entire courtroom, including Judge VanCulver, stood as Mr. Evans led the jurors to the jury box.

Judge VanCulver smiled at the jurors. "Good morning. I trust you all slept comfortably at the hotel."

Judge VanCulver explained to the jurors that they would hear opening statements from each attorney, then they would present their case.

The court stenographer, Candace, a full-figured brunette, situated her hands and was ready to type.

"Ms. Connors, you may proceed with your opening statement." Judge instructed.

"Thank you." Inez stood.

Inez walked over to the jury box, smiled and began to speak to the jurors. "Good morning, ladies and gentlemen of the jury. My name is Inez Connors. I am the attorney for the plaintiff," she pointed, "Beverly Monday."

She walked over to the lectern. She thanked them for serving and expressed her apologies for taking them away from their families. "This case is about a little boy. His name is Bryce Monday. Bryce was born cognitively disabled. His brain was half the size of a normal infant."

The jurors were attentive and so was Judge VanCulver. Inez pointed at Beverly again. "We're here today because Bryce's mother received a call from the teacher's union representative informing her that her son was physically abused. He was abused not once, not twice, but at least three times, by his teacher, Jennifer Reinhart." Inez stared at Jennifer who sat with her hands in her lap.

Inez continued. "You're going to hear Bryce's mother testify that she saw a bruise on her son's back. She doesn't know where it came from, but I will show you, ladies and gentlemen of the jury, through testimony of the witnesses, that Bryce Monday received the bruise from his teacher," she pointed, "Jennifer Reinhart."

A tear rolled down Beverly's cheek.

Inez examined the faces of the jurors. "You're going to hear witnesses tell you how they saw Jennifer Reinhart inflict such horrific pain upon Bryce Monday that he screamed in agony."

The jurors' expressions were sad and juror number two, Annie Mae Wallace, the only black juror, rolled her eyes in Jennifer's direction. Douglas doodled as if nothing mattered.

Inez proceeded. "Ladies and gentlemen of the jury, you're going to hear testimony that when the abuse was reported to the principal," she glanced at Robert Clayborn, "he did absolutely nothing to help this poor defenseless child. He didn't even have the decency to inform my client."

Inez left the lectern, paced from one end of the jury box to the other end, then back to the lectern. "You're going to hear testimony about the training and qualifications needed to teach a child like Bryce Monday. Jennifer Reinhart did not have those qualifications." Inez darted a glance at Mora Abernathy. "Despite the fact Ms. Reinhart was not qualified, she was still hired by Melbourne Public School System."

Judge VanCulver still seemed attentive. Martin patted Beverly on the shoulder and Joey gave her a tissue.

Jennifer slouched in her seat for a moment. She leaned forward, placed both elbows on the table and rested her chin in her hands. Robert stared over his shoulder at his wife then at Inez. Mora sat with her legs crossed at the knee and glared at Inez.

Ella Walker smiled, head held high, apparently glad that Jennifer and Robert were on trial.

Inez appeared confident that the jury had sympathy for Bryce. "Bryce is eight years old. Any normal child could tell his mother someone was hurting him. Bryce's disabilities wouldn't allow him to do that. A behavior psychologist will tell you Bryce's mental capacity ranges between the ages of eight months to one year and there was no way he could communicate to anyone the torture he endured."

Douglas' doodling appeared to have turned into writing, obviously he decided to take notes. He sighed a few times but definitely seemed impressed with Inez's opening remarks.

The courtroom was silent. Tears flowed steadily down Beverly's face. Martin leaned forward to comfort her.

It was obvious Inez's opening statement had captured concern from the entire courtroom. She concluded with, "Ladies and gentlemen of the jury, after you've heard all the testimonies you'll see that Bryce Monday's civil rights were violated and school officials did nothing to help this child. Once the evidence is in, I know you'll render a verdict of guilty."

Joey handed Beverly another tissue. The jurors watched with empathy.

Inez left the lectern and walked up to the jury box again. "And now, ladies and gentlemen of the jury, I want you to meet Bryce Monday." Inez walked to the back of the courtroom and opened the door. Sharon entered, holding Bryce's hand. Sharon placed Bryce's hand in Inez's. Inez led Bryce up to the jury box so the jurors could get a good look at him.

Beverly wiped her tears and smiled at Bryce as he stared into space.

Inez walked Bryce from one end of the jury box to the other. Bryce continued to gaze. Twelve sympathetic smiles captured the attention of the entire courtroom. Inez then led Bryce to the back of the courtroom.

One of the jurors, Denise Thatcher, leaned over the jury box and watched Bryce's feet as he stumbled a couple of times when Inez led him back to Sharon. Sharon took Bryce out of the courtroom.

Inez scored points with the jury. She stared at Douglas on her way back to the front of the courtroom. Douglas watched her with determination.

Inez once again approached the jury. "Thank you ladies and gentlemen of the jury." She sat down.

Judge VanCulver looked at Douglas. "Opening remarks, Mr. Pratt."

Douglas stood, brushed the sleeves of his black suit and straightened the collar of his custom made shirt. "Yes, thank you, your Honor."

Slowly, Douglas neared the lectern. "Good morning ladies and gentlemen. My name is Douglas Pratt and I represent the defendants, Jennifer Reinhart, Robert Clayborn, and Mora Abernathy who is here on behalf of Melbourne Public School System."

Douglas cleared his throat. "This case is being brought to you by a concerned mother. Any parent who is told their child has been abused should be concerned. I know I'd want to find out what really happened if it were my child. Ms. Monday should be concerned."

Douglas glanced compassionately at Beverly, then back to the jurors.

Inez wrote on her notepad, passed it to Joey. The note said, *it would be nice to have some bread to go with that baloney.* Joey smiled. Beverly read the note as it passed and smiled.

Douglas continued. "You met Bryce Monday, and it's obvious that he's in need of special care and attention, which is what his teacher," he looked in the defendant's direction, "Jennifer Reinhart gave him, and that's what my client will tell you. You'll hear testimony to convince you these charges were drummed up out of anger at Jennifer Reinhart. You'll also hear testimony that will prove Robert Clayborn is a victim because of problems with employees and because of his interracial marriage; all of which are totally unrelated to this case."

Douglas left the lectern and walked from one end of the jury box to the other end. "Jennifer Reinhart was qualified. She did not hurt Bryce Monday. Ladies and gentlemen of the jury, after you've heard the testimonies, you'll know no abuse took place. This innocent child was used in an effort to retaliate against school officials because of personal dislike. Ladies and gentlemen, it will be obvious after the evidence is in. I know you'll deliver a verdict of not guilty. Thank you."

Judge VanCulver appeared surprised that Mr. Pratt's opening remarks were brief. Judge VanCulver turned toward Inez. "You may call your first witness, Ms. Connors."

"Thank you. I call Mrs. Ella Walker to the stand."

Ella stood and walked up to the front.

Mr. Evans met her at the witness stand with the Bible. Ella placed her right hand on the Bible and repeated after Mr. Evans. "I promise to tell the truth, the whole truth, nothing but the truth." Ella's eyes shifted towards Jennifer and Mr. Clayborn, "so help me God." She sat down, brushed the few gray strands of hair from her face.

Inez stood and walked to the witness box. "State your full name, please."

"Ella Dee Walker."

"And where are you employed, Mrs. Walker?"

"Carter Elementary School."

"In what capacity?"

"I'm a Handicapped Children's Assistant."

"What exactly is a Handicapped Children's Assistant?"

"I assist the teacher in the classroom. I'm an aide."

"Mrs. Walker, what are some of the duties you perform?"

"I help the children eat. I help them use the bathroom because they aren't potty trained and I change their diapers. I help look out for them. Some people say it's like babysitting, but it's a lot more involved than that."

"Was Bryce Monday in your class?"

"Yes."

"Tell us about Bryce."

"Bryce is a loveable little boy and he didn't deserve what Jennifer did to him."

Douglas jumped to his feet and yelled, "I object, your Honor. The witness was not asked a question about my client."

Judge VanCulver peered over his glasses at Ella. "Just answer the questions you're asked, Mrs. Walker."

Ella nodded. "Yes Sir."

"Proceed Counselor." Judge VanCulver said to Inez.

"Mrs. Walker, you spoke to the principal, Robert Clayborn, back in March of this year. Is that correct?"

"Yes."

Please tell the jury why you went to the principal's office."

Ella looked at the jury. "I went to see Mr. Clayborn because I didn't like the way Jennifer Reinhart treated Bryce Monday."

"Who is Jennifer Reinhart?" Inez asked.

"Bryce Monday's teacher."

"Is she here today?"

"Yes." Ella pointed.

"Is the principal, Robert Clayborn, here?"

"Yes." Ella pointed.

Inez looked at Judge VanCulver. "Please let the record show that Ella Walker identified the defendants, Jennifer Reinhart and Robert Clayborn. Continue Mrs. Walker."

"I told Mr. Clayborn that Jennifer twisted Bryce's arms and pushed his face to the floor. She put her knee in his back."

"Did Bryce have a tantrum?"

"No, he did not have a tantrum."

"What provoked Ms. Reinhart into doing this?"

"Bryce didn't like to drink milk from a cup. Bryce's mother explained this to me and Jennifer on the first day of school. Jennifer told his mother that she didn't have a problem with that. But she was determined to make him drink from a cup."

"What would Ms. Reinhart do to Bryce?"

"She would twist his arms and push his face to the floor."

"What would Bryce do?"

"He would scream because it hurt."

Beverly burst into tears as she listened to Ella testify to how Jennifer handled her son with force. Joey held Beverly's hand and Martin sprung forward and wrapped his arms around her from behind.

Inez went back to her table and Joey handed her a life-size doll of Bryce.

"Your Honor I would like to enter this doll as Exhibit A."

Judge VanCulver looked at Douglas. Douglas nodded in agreement.

"Mrs. Walker, I would like you to step down and show the jury exactly what Ms. Reinhart did to Bryce Monday. I'd like you to use this doll."

Ella stepped down, took the doll and stood in front of the jury. Ella laid the doll face down, pulled the arms behind its back and distorted her face as she applied pressure.

Beverly's trembling hand wiped her tears. She closed her eyes tight and shook her head.

Jennifer stared at Ella while Robert didn't raise his head. Mora uncrossed then crossed her legs again.

Douglas folded his arms and looked at everything in the courtroom except Ella. He shot a glare at the pictures of Abraham Lincoln and George Washington that hung side by side on the beige wall behind the Judge. The United States of America flag that was mounted on the wall behind the Judge suddenly became of interest.

Ella spoke fast and breathlessly. "When Bryce stopped breathing, Jennifer stood him up, put her arms around him from behind," she demonstrated.

"Then what happened?" Inez asked.

"Jennifer would start to sing Ring Around The Rosies to calm him down. After a few seconds the color came back to Bryce's face and he started breathing normal."

The jurors appeared stunned. One of the jurors, Denise Thatcher, removed her glasses and wiped her eyes. Annie Mae Wallace stared down at the floor and shook her head.

Beverly rubbed her temples. Her eyes flooded with tears.

Inez took the doll and instructed Ella to return to the witness stand. "Did you report this incident?"

"Yes."

"To whom?"

I told the principal, Robert Clayborn."

"What happened when you told Mr. Clayborn."

"He said he would talk to Jennifer and have a meeting with Bryce's mother."

"And did he?"

"He talked to Jennifer."

"Did Mr. Clayborn meet with Bryce's mother?"

"No."

"Why not?"

"Mr. Clayborn said that when he talked to Jennifer, he was satisfied abuse had not taken place. He said he was not going to contact Bryce's mother because he believed nothing happened."

"What did you do?"

"I told Mr. Clayborn I would do something if he didn't. He said he didn't want any more trouble because he already had grievances filed against him." Ella frowned. "Mr. Clayborn said that since Bryce was going to a different school in fall, it didn't matter."

"What else did Mr. Clayborn say?"

Douglas stood up immediately. "Objection. Ms. Connors is leading the witness."

"Sustained."

Inez grinned. "I'll rephrase the question, Your Honor."

"Mrs. Walker, was that the end of your conversation with Mr. Clayborn?"

"No."

"What else?"

"Mr. Clayborn told me my six month performance review was coming up soon. He reminded me other qualified people had applied for my job. I know he was threatening me to keep quiet or he'd fire me."

Douglas sprang to his feet. "Objection. The witness is speculating. She has no way of knowing what his thoughts were. She's not a mind reader."

"Sustained. The jury will disregard the witness's last remarks." Judge looked at Candace. "Strike Mrs. Walker's last remark from the record." He turned to Inez. "Continue, Ms. Connors."

Robert Clayborn leaned over and whispered in Jennifer's ear. Perhaps to ask Jennifer if she really did do those horrible things to Bryce. If so, it was a bit too late.

"What happened next, Mrs. Walker?"

"I contacted the Melbourne Teacher's Union and reported the abuse to Jeffrey Garrison and Mr. Garrison told Bryce's mother."

Inez returned to the plaintiff's table and Joey handed her a document and she gave it to Ella. "Only a couple more questions, Mrs. Walker. Did you write this letter to the teacher's union?"

"Yes I did."

"Please read the letter to the jury."

Ella read.

> "Dear Mr. Garrison:
>
> I am writing this letter because I don't know what else to do. Bryce Monday is a cognitively disabled child in the classroom where I work at Carter Elementary School. The teacher, Jennifer Reinhart, has been physically abusing him since March of this year. The child screams in pain. She pushed his face to the

floor. She drags him by his legs. She's even yanked his ears. I fear for his life. I contacted the principal at Carter, Mr. Robert Clayborn, and he refuses to do anything. This has to stop before she kills this child. Please help.

Sincerely,
Ella Walker"

Beverly wiped the tears from her puffy red eyes.

Inez took the letter from Ella. "Did you do or say anything to Ms. Reinhart when she was abusing Bryce?"

Douglas yelled, "Objection!"

"Overruled, you may continue." Judge VanCulver said.

Inez looked at Douglas and smirked. "Answer the question, Mrs. Walker. Did you do or say anything when Jennifer Reinhart was abusing Bryce Monday?"

"Yes."

"Please tell the court."

"When Jennifer had Bryce on the floor, I told her he wasn't breathing and she was going to kill him."

"And what did Ms. Reinhart say?"

"Jennifer told me you have to let these kids know who's in charge. She also told me that she wanted me to do the same thing to Bryce and I refused. That's why I reported her because I'm not going to handle any child like that."

"Were there any other times Ms. Reinhart had a confrontation with Bryce Monday?"

"Yes. Bryce was drooling and she called him a rabid dog. She wiped his mouth so hard he started to kick. She grabbed him by his ears and the poor child started to scream."

Murmurs filled the courtroom. Beverly cried out and buried her face in her hands.

Judge VanCulver banged his gavel and the court became silent once again. He looked at Beverly. "Ma'am, I know this is difficult for you, but I cannot have these outbursts in my court. Would you like a few minutes to gain your composure?"

Beverly wiped her nose and eyes and shook her head.

"Very well, continue Counselor."

"Your Honor, I have no further questions. Thank you, Mrs. Walker."

"Cross examine, Mr. Pratt?" Judge VanCulver asked.

Douglas stood and walked to the lectern and stared at Ella. She tightened her lips and held her head up high. Ella was ready for Douglas.

"Mrs. Walker, how long have you been at Carter Elementary School?"

"About ten months now."

"Prior to the end of the school year, did you receive your six month performance review?"

"Yes."

Douglas returned to his table, picked up a piece of paper, showed it to Inez then handed it to Ella. "Tell the jury what this is?"

"It's a copy of my performance review?"

"Read what it says in the remarks area."

Ella read.

"Mrs. Walker continues to undermine my authority with the children. She's uncooperative and doesn't follow instructions. She has a poor attitude which makes her extremely difficult to work with."

Douglas took the evaluation from Ella. "Mrs. Walker, who wrote your performance review?"

"Jennifer Reinhart."

"Did you report Ms. Reinhart to the union before or after your review?"

Inez stood. "Your Honor, I object."

"Overruled. Answer the question." Judge ordered.

Douglas repeated. "Was it before or after, Mrs. Walker?"

"It was after."

"You reported the alleged abuse to the union after you received your performance review. You were trying to retaliate against Ms. Reinhart because you didn't agree with the review she gave you." Douglas yelled, "In fact, you were furious."

Inez lunged out of her chair. "Your Honor, I must object. Mrs. Walker's evaluation or her relationship with the defendant has nothing to do with this case."

"Overruled."

Beverly scowled at Douglas.

Douglas gaped at Ella. "Mrs. Walker, you claim you went to Robert Clayborn and he did nothing. Then why didn't you call the police if Bryce Monday was being abused?"

Still calm, Ella said, "It was not my job. I followed procedure."

"But child abuse?" Douglas asked. "Even if you didn't call the police, why didn't you at least tell Bryce's mother?"

He threw his hands in the air. "To hell with procedure. If this woman was abusing a child, you should've done more than just go to the principal's office."

Inez jumped to her feet. "Your Honor, Mr. Pratt is badgering the witness."

Judge VanCulver peered over his glasses at Douglas. "Mr. Pratt, you've been in my courtroom enough times to know that I don't tolerate grandstanding."

Douglas smiled. "I apologize, Your Honor."

Douglas turned to Ella. "Mrs. Walker, I just want to make sure that it's real clear to the court what happened."

Still unyielding, Ella said, "It was not my job. I followed procedure."

"You didn't call the police. You didn't tell Bryce's mother."

"I told you, Sir, I followed procedure and procedure is to go to the principal."

"I'm sorry, Mrs. Walker, but if a child's being abused, you should've gone to the police, but instead, you told a union representative." Sarcastically, he added, "and then only after you received a bad performance review." Douglas stared at the jury. "I think the jury understands. No further questions."

Judge VanCulver studied his watch. "Now would be a good time to adjourn for lunch."

* * *

The court cafeteria didn't have the greatest food, but it was close and Judge VanCulver only allowed one hour for lunch. Inez, Joey and Ella went to the cafeteria. Beverly and Martin skipped lunch and decided to go over to Sharon's to check on Bryce.

Inez ordered a chicken salad on whole wheat, Joey ordered tuna and Ella ordered chili.

Joey took a huge bite of his sandwich. "I think you did good, Ella. Don't you, Inez?"

Inez nibbled at her sandwich. "Yeah, Pratt tried to rattle you, but you stayed firm."

Ella scooped a spoonful of her piping hot chili and blew on it. "I knew he was trying to make it seem like I made it all up because I got a bad review."

Joey grabbed the other half of his sandwich. "So who are you going to call this afternoon?"

"Dr. Alice Thrasher and, if there's enough time, Agnes Harris. I informed both of them to be here this afternoon."

* * *

Beverly and Martin arrived at Sharon's. Sharon was washing dishes. Bryce sat at the breakfast nook in the kitchen and watched his Uncle Tyler fill the bowls with chocolate ice cream.

Sharon dried her hands on the dish towel to open the door for Beverly. "Why did you come to the back door?"

Martin and Beverly entered. Beverly walked over to Bryce and kissed him and sat down. "Because I knew you'd be in the kitchen having lunch."

Martin walked over and picked Bryce up and sat in the chair, with Bryce on his lap. "How's my big guy?"

Bryce smiled and hugged Martin.

Sharon joined them at the table. "We just finished lunch and was about to have some ice cream."

Martin kissed Bryce on top of his head. "Tyler, give me Bryce's bowl, I'll feed him."

"Martin, do you and Beverly want some lunch?" Tyler asked.

Beverly signed. "No, thanks. I'm not hungry."

"None for me either." Martin said.

Sharon ate a spoonful of ice cream. "I made burgers, there's plenty of ground beef left."

"No thanks, Sis."

Martin fed Bryce a spoonful of ice cream.

Beverly smiled. "You're so good with him. He really loves you, Martin."

"I love him too."

Tyler asked, "How did it go in court this morning?"

Beverly rubbed her temples. "I don't like that other attorney. He's twisting everything around."

Sharon stopped eating. "When Ms. Connors took Bryce to the front of the courtroom so the jury could see him, it really looked like they sympathized with him." I think Bryce made an impression on all of the jurors."

Martin nodded. "I agree. That was definitely a plus for us. Pratt is good. He definitely knows his way around the courtroom. But so does Inez."

Tyler smiled at Beverly. "Everything's going to be okay. You'll see."

"Thanks, brother-in-law. I think I need some glue because I am using every ounce of my strength to keep my ass in the chair. I'm doing all I can to keep from grabbing that bitch."

Martin put his hands over Bryce's ears. "Calm down, baby, I know how you feel. You have to keep your composure. Don't let her get to you. I know it's hard, but you've got to try. We both have to try."

Beverly covered her mouth with her hand. "Excuse my language. I'm sorry."

Sharon rubbed Beverly's arm. "I know how you feel. When I saw that fat cow I felt like snatching her ass out of that chair. Let's not even mention the principal. He's just pitiful. How can you know someone is hurting a child and not do shit?"

"Ladies, calm down." Tyler said. "I don't understand why Bryce isn't in the courtroom for the whole trial." Tyler looked at Martin. "I'm no attorney, but wouldn't it be good for the jurors to see him throughout the trial?"

Martin nodded. "I'm sure Inez will have Sharon bring him back to court again. If Bryce could testify, he would. But children get restless, and especially Bryce."

Sharon hugged Beverly. "All of them will get exactly what they deserve. It's only a matter of time."

Martin looked at the white sun-shaped clock that hung over the bay window in the kitchen. "Speaking of time, it's almost one-fifteen. We'd better get back to court."

* * *

Court reconvened at one-thirty in the afternoon and Inez called Dr. Alice Thrasher to the stand.

Dr. Thrasher's blonde hair was pulled back from her face and was twisted in a ball that rested at the back of her head. Her make up concealed most of her wrinkled skin. Her wire frame glasses on a chain, rested on her chest. The skirt to her gray suit came well below her knee. She approached the witness stand holding a small brown notepad in her hand.

"State your full name." Inez said.

"Alice Lynette Thrasher."

"What is your profession?"

"I'm a doctor specializing in behavior psychology. My main focus is children who are cognitively disabled."

"Where do you live?"

"I live in Menomonee, Wisconsin."

"Are you licensed in Wisconsin?"

"Yes."

"When did you receive your license in Wisconsin?"

"January, 1971."

"Where did you receive your education?"

"I acquired my Bachelor's Degree from the University of Menomonee and my Doctrine of Medicine from the University of Melbourne." "You said you specialize in behavior psychology, focusing mainly on cognitively disabled children?"

"Correct."

"Dr. Thrasher, please tell the jury what that means."

Dr. Thrasher kept her hands in her lap and spoke directly to the jury. "A behavior disorder is any type of behavior that goes to an outer limit. These are behaviors that repeatedly break society's expectations."

"Now, Dr. Thrasher, you had the opportunity to evaluate Bryce Monday?"

"Yes."

"What is your medical opinion of Bryce Monday?"

Dr. Thrasher flipped through the pages of her notepad. "Bryce was born with microencephaly. Microencephaly is any person with an unusually small head. Micro means small and encephaly is head or brain. The brain is small and underdeveloped as with Bryce Monday. People born with this condition are cognitively disabled. Mentally they are years behind others their age. In some cases, depending upon the severity of the malformation of the brain, individuals with this condition may or may not speak or walk."

"Doctor, how has Bryce's disability affected him?"

"Bryce is eight years old. His mental capacity is that of a twelve-month to eighteen-month old baby. He can walk, but with difficulty because of the way his feet turn inward. His gross motor skills have been extremely affected by his birth defect. He can't communicate. He said the word, 'no' and 'mommy'. It was not distinct. He cannot button, unbutton or tie his shoes."

"Did Bryce ever become angry during your interview?"

"Absolutely not."

"How did Bryce react?"

"Actually he was quite affectionate. He likes to hug."

"If you had to restrain a child who was obviously out of control with the same disabilities as Bryce, how would you do that?"

"It all depends on what the child was doing. If the child was trying to hit me, I would hold him from behind with his arms crossed in front of his body."

"Did you think Bryce was violent?"

"No."

"Have you ever seen cases where a child of Bryce's mental capacity needed to be restrained on the floor?"

"Yes."

"Tell the jury."

Dr. Thrasher looked at the jury. "If a child is hitting, one way to restrain the child would be to bring the child to the floor and sit the child between your legs with your arms around the child from behind. You would hold the child in this position until he or she calms down."

"I have no further questions."

Douglas stood as Inez sat. "Dr. Thrasher, have you ever spent a whole day in a classroom full of children like Bryce Monday?"

"No."

"Just one-on-one?"

"Yes."

Douglas wanted to make sure the jury understood Dr. Thrasher had only related with children one at a time, which was quite different than dealing with several at a time. "So just because Bryce didn't become violent with you, doesn't mean that he's never been violent."

"True."

"No further questions."

Judge VanCulver exhaled. "Due to the late hour, I'm going to adjourn." He banged his gavel. "Court is adjourned until nine a.m. tomorrow."

* * *

Inez spent the evening reading over statements and questions for day two of the trial. She put on her pink satin gown and crawled into bed. Her bed was covered with law books, papers and questions for each witness.

She was pleased with the outcome of the first day. Ella Walker was fantastic and definitely had the jury on her side. Inez felt sorry for Beverly when she burst into tears. It was the first time Beverly had seen a demonstration of how Bryce was abused.

The jury didn't seem bothered Ella never called the police and that she didn't tell Bryce's mother. She read over the material until about two a.m.

Inez tried to come up with every imaginable question Douglas might even remotely ask. She knew he was too laid back because he only had three objections. It definitely wasn't like the Douglas Pratt she knew.

Inez's eyes blurred and she developed a headache. She put her head back on the pillow and fell asleep surrounded by her books and papers.

CHAPTER TWENTY-ONE

Court began promptly at nine a.m. After the jury entered, Judge VanCulver addressed them. "I trust you all rested comfortably last night in the hotel. I know it's not home but, under the circumstances, I hope it wasn't too bad."

One of the jurors, Laurel Valentine, removed her wire frame glasses and massaged her temple. Another juror, Dominic Santiago, scratched his thick sideburn. The young brunette with a blonde streak, Tianna Adams, folded her arms and smiled.

"Call your next witness." Judge VanCulver instructed Inez.

Inez stood. "I call Agnes Harris to the stand."

Agnes waddled to the stand balancing her weight as best she could. She plopped in the chair, after being sworn in. Sweat dribbled down the side of her face.

"State your full name for the record." Inez said.

"Agnes Harris."

"Where are you employed?"

"Carter Elementary School."

"Are you married?"

"No, I'm single."

"What is your occupation, Ms. Harris?"

"I teach third grade."

"What education do you have?"

"I have a Bachelor's Degree in education."

"Are you familiar with the children in the cognitively disabled classroom at Carter Elementary?"

"I don't interact with them, but I know who they are."

"Do you know Bryce Monday?"

"Yes, Ma'am."

"How do you know him?"

"Bryce is one of the children in the cognitively disabled classroom."

"Do you know Jennifer Reinhart?" Inez pointed.

"Yes. Jennifer is the teacher in Bryce's class."

"Do you know Ella Walker?"

Agnes looked at Ella. "Yes, I do. Ella is the aide in Bryce's class."

"Ms. Harris, you wrote a letter to the union regarding Bryce Monday?"

Agnes sighed. "Yes, Lord, I did."

Inez returned to her table and gave Agnes a sheet of paper. Douglas already had a copy in hand.

"Is this your statement?" Inez questioned.

"Yes, it is."

"Please read to the jury what you wrote."

Agnes cleared her throat.

> "Dear Mr. Garrison:
>
> "I was coming out of the gym with my students and as I turned the corner, I saw Jennifer Reinhart holding Bryce Monday's hand. Ms. Reinhart started to squeeze Bryce's hand. I heard her say, walk faster, dammit. Ms. Reinhart yanked Bryce by the hand. She squeezed his hand so hard he screamed. When Ms. Reinhart saw me she stopped and started humming Ring Around The Rosies. This is not the proper way to treat a child and I'm writing to you because this issue should be addressed. Bryce Monday is handicapped and can't walk very fast because he is pigeon toed. Please look into this matter. Thank you.
>
> Sincerely,
> Agnes Harris"

Beverly's head dropped and she wiped the tears from her face. She rolled her eyes at Jennifer. Jennifer picked her nails as if she really didn't give a damn.

Robert stared blankly at Agnes.

Mora Abernathy's leg dangled, crossed at the knee, with her arms folded.

Douglas watched Agnes eagerly as he waited for his turn to cross-examine.

Inez grabbed the replica of Bryce and handed it to Agnes.

"Ms. Harris, I would like you to stand and show the jury what you saw Jennifer Reinhart do to Bryce Monday."

Douglas stood. "Your Honor, I object."

"Overruled."

Inez repeated. "Ms. Harris, I would like you to stand and demonstrate for the jury what you saw."

Agnes took the doll and squeezed the doll's hand with both her hands. She frowned as she applied as much pressure as she could, biting down on her bottom lip.

The jurors winced as if they could feel the pain that Bryce endured.

A woman in the back of the courtroom yelled, "Oh, sweet Jesus."

Beverly burst into tears again and was calmed by Joey and Martin.

Judge banged his gavel. "Quiet in the courtroom."

Inez was pleased with the influence Ms. Harris' demonstration had on the entire courtroom. Beverly's tears made it better for her case.

Inez took the doll. "Thank you, Ms. Harris. I have no further questions."

Douglas stood and started towards the lectern before Judge VanCulver could ask if he wanted to cross-examine.

"Go ahead, Mr. Pratt." Judge said.

Douglas walked up to Agnes and rested his palms on the witness box. "Ms. Harris did you say anything to Ms. Reinhart when you saw her with Bryce?"

"No."

"Did you call the police?"

"No, Sir."

"Did you tell Bryce's mother?"

"No, I did not."

Snidely, Douglas said, "Well, I'm afraid I don't understand. Do you always ignore child abuse?"

Inez shouted. "Your Honor, I object!"

"Sustained." Judge VanCulver said. "You know better, Mr. Pratt."

"I'm sorry, Your Honor." Douglas cleared his throat. "Ms. Harris, why didn't you say something?" He hollered. "For God's sake, why didn't you call the police?"

Inez yelled, "Your Honor, please."

Judge VanCulver rapped his gavel above the chatter in the courtroom. "Silence in the court. Mr. Pratt, I'm warning you. I won't tolerate your behavior."

"Sorry, Judge."

The jurors didn't seem to appreciate Pratt's behavior. One juror, Maxwell Cane, shook his head and frowned.

"Ms. Harris, you claim Jennifer Reinhart inflicted pain upon Bryce Monday. You didn't call the police, you didn't tell Bryce's mother and you never said anything to Ms. Reinhart. If a child was being abused, it was your duty to do something. You could have told Ms. Reinhart to stop hurting Bryce. You could have done something to help Bryce. All you did was write a letter to the union. Correct?"

Calmly, eye to eye, Ms. Harris said, "Correct."

Inez looked over at the jury and their expressions were that of confusion. They were probably wondering the same thing.

Douglas continued. "Ms. Harris, you filed a grievance against Robert Clayborn in March of this year?"

"Yes, I did."

"What was the reason for the grievance?"

Inez rose to her feet. "I object, Your Honor. Ms. Harris' grievance has no bearing on the case."

"I'll allow the question. Answer the question Ms. Harris." Judge VanCulver instructed.

"I filed a reverse discrimination grievance against Mr. Clayborn."

"Tell the jury why you filed this particular type of grievance."

Ms. Harris looked at the predominantly white jury. "I filed a complaint against Mr. Clayborn because he treats the white teachers better than the black teachers."

"How did he discriminate against you?"

Inez sprung to her feet. "Your Honor, I must object. The details of Ms. Harris' grievance have nothing to do with what she witnessed. It is totally irrelevant and Mr. Pratt knows it."

Douglas turned towards Inez, then to Judge VanCulver. "With all due respect, Your Honor, I intend to show that there is a connection."

"Mr. Pratt, you'd better proceed with caution. I mean it."

"Thank you, Your Honor. Answer the question Ms. Harris," Douglas instructed.

Inez looked at Judge VanCulver and thought to herself. *How could the bald headed son-of-a-bitch let Pratt the prick continue with this unrelated line of questioning.*

"Could you repeat the question, please?" Ms. Harris asked.

"How did Mr. Clayborn discriminate against you?"

"Mr. Clayborn would not allow me to teach the children in my class about the Bible, but he allowed a white teacher to teach prayers to the children in her classroom."

"Did you ask him why?"

"Yes."

"What did he say?"

"He said he was in charge and he felt it was best. That was all the explanation he would give me."

"Were you upset?"

"Yes, of course, I was."

"Ms. Harris, you were so upset that you wrote this letter to get back at Mr. Clayborn. You accused Ms. Reinhart of abuse, but you also knew Ella Walker was going to claim that Mr. Clayborn did nothing to stop the abuse which would make him indirectly responsible."

Ella leaned forward and squinted at Douglas. He was doing to Agnes what he'd done to her.

"No, that's not true." Agnes replied.

"You want to ruin the reputation of a man because you couldn't have your way."

Breathing faster, Agnes yelled. "I'm not lying. That woman squeezed Bryce's hand." Agnes raised her hand in the air. "As God is my witness, she did it."

Douglas looked at the jury, threw his hands up in the air. "I have no further questions of this witness."

Jennifer and Robert smiled for the first time. Robert looked over his shoulder and smiled at Susan.

Beverly reached over her shoulder. Martin grasped her hand.

Judge VanCulver recessed court until one-thirty p.m.

CHAPTER TWENTY-TWO

The weather had made a drastic change by the afternoon. What started out as a sunny sixty-three degrees, ended up rainy, gloomy, coupled with thunder and lightning. The clouds were gray and by one o'clock in the afternoon it was as dark as midnight. The air had an unusual sensation to the skin. The cool breeze was normal for October in Melbourne, but the muggy feeling suggested a windstorm.

A tornado warning was issued at one-fifteen by the City of Melbourne Weather Bureau.

Despite the weather, Judge VanCulver started on time. "Call your next witness," he instructed Inez.

Inez stood. "I call Mr. Galen Small to the stand."

Galen briskly strutted up to the witness stand. He seemed to be in a hurry to tell his story. Galen stared at Douglas, Robert Clayborn and Jennifer Reinhart as he pranced to the witness stand. Galen swore to tell the truth and sat down. He tucked his blazing red shirt in his navy blue slacks.

"State your full name please," Inez said.

"Galen Michael Small."

"Where are you employed, Mr. Small?"

"Carter Elementary School."

"What is your position at Carter Elementary School?"

"I'm the assistant librarian."

"Do you know Bryce Monday?"

"Yeah. I know who he is."

"Do you know Jennifer Reinhart?"

"Yeah, she's Bryce's teacher?"

"Mr. Small, you encountered Ms. Reinhart and Bryce one afternoon. Is that correct?"

"Yeah."

"When?"

"It was right before summer vacation. I would say around the end of May, beginning of June this year."

"Please tell the jury what happened."

Galen did not look at the jury. He continued to talk to Inez. "I heard noises like a grunt or a scuffle. It was a muffled sound. It was like somebody was screaming with their hand over their mouth," he demonstrated. "I looked around the corner and I saw Jennifer Reinhart and Bryce Monday."

"What were they doing?"

"Jennifer had Bryce down on the stairs, face down. She was shoving his face to the floor. Jennifer put her knee in his back and pushed really hard."

"How do you know it was hard, Mr. Small?"

"Because Jennifer was biting on her lip and grunting. She was applying pressure. Bryce attempted to lift his head. That's when I saw his lip had started to bleed from being pressed to the floor. She was too strong for the little guy."

Beverly sobbed and began to cough.

Judge VanCulver removed his glasses. "Are you alright? Would you like a few moments?"

Beverly's teary eyes glanced at Judge VanCulver. "No." She mumbled.

"Very well. You may continue, Ms. Connors." Judge VanCulver said. Inez handed Galen his statement. "Mr. Small is that your handwriting?"

"Yeah. I wrote this to the union representative. It basically says what I just said about how Jennifer hurt Bryce."

"Please read it to the jury."

Galen continued to face Inez.

> *"Dear Mr. Garrison:*
>
> *I work at Carter Elementary School. I saw the handicap teacher, Jennifer Reinhart, on the stairs one day with one of the kids, Bryce Monday. Jennifer Reinhart pushed Bryce's face down*

on the stairs. She made his lip bleed. She used way too much force on this little kid. She put her knee in his back. Bryce was in pain. Bryce is little for his age and it's obvious he was born handicapped. I don't know much about these kind of kids, but this is abuse and I hope you can do something so that this stops.

Sincerely,
Galen Small"

Judge VanCulver was writing. It was hard to tell if he was paying attention or if he was doodling.

Whispers echoed throughout the courtroom.

Beverly bowed her head and wept. Martin put his arms around her.

Douglas slouched in his chair and twirled his pen. Galen had the jury's undivided attention.

Inez got the doll and handed it to Galen. "Mr. Small, would you please step down and show the jury what Ms. Reinhart did to Bryce?"

"With pleasure."

Galen demonstrated with great force on the doll.

Douglas examined the reactions of the jurors.

Two of the jurors in the front row, Margaret Lewis and Louis DeChambre, leaned forward, eyebrows raised and watched intensely. Another juror, Ruth Beckom, shook her head in horror. Still another juror, John Williams eyes widened, his mouth dropped open, obviously upset by what Bryce had endured.

Beverly burst into tears and stood to exit. She couldn't stand to watch. Martin gently grabbed her by the arm and pulled her over to him and sat her down next to him. He put his arms around her. Beverly laid her head on Martin's chest and cried profusely. "Martin, I asked her about his busted lip and she told me he fell."

Ella shook her head at Jennifer.

The crack of thunder shook the entire courtroom.

Someone in the courtroom yelled, "Oh my God." Another voice yelled, "Have mercy, Jesus."

Expressionless, Jennifer watched Galen. It was hard to tell what she thought or how she felt.

Mr. Clayborn seemed sympathetic.

Judge VanCulver banged his gavel to quiet his courtroom.

Inez took the doll from Galen and instructed him to return to the witness stand. "Mr. Small, what happened next?"

"I asked Jennifer Reinhart what was she doing to Bryce?"

"What was Ms. Reinhart's response?"

"She told me to stick to my books and mind my own business. She said you have to handle these kids like that."

"What happened next?"

"I don't know much about handicapped kids so I believed her. Especially when she told me Mrs. Walker had to handle Bryce like that."

Ella jumped out of her seat. "And that's a lie because I would never do that to a child."

Judge VanCulver yelled. "Silence. Take your seat immediately. Another outburst from you, Madam, and I'll have you removed from my court."

Ella glared at Jennifer as she sat down.

Jennifer never acknowledged Ella's flare-up. She focused intently on the bronze round emblem in the front center of the Judge's bench that said *State of Wisconsin.*

Inez peered at the jurors then at Judge VanCulver. "I have no further questions of this witness."

Douglas grinned at Inez as if to say, "Bravo, Ms. Connors."

Judge VanCulver turned to Douglas. "Cross-examine?"

Douglas stood and walked to the witness box. "Mr. Small, did you file a reverse discrimination grievance against Robert Clayborn?"

"Yeah, I did."

"You filed that grievance because you applied for the position of head librarian and Mr. Clayborn gave it to another employee. Isn't that true?"

With a bit of sarcasm Galen said, "So what if he did."

"That other employee was white, wasn't she?" Douglas asked.

"Yeah, she was."

Inez stood. "Your Honor, this has no bearing on this case."

"Overruled."

"Mr. Small, did you receive a verbal warning last year because you were encouraging the black children not to play with the white children?"

"That ain't got nothing to do with what I saw."

"Your Honor, please instruct the witness to answer the question."

Judge VanCulver leaned over the bench. "Mr. Small, answer Mr. Pratt's question."

"But it don't have anything to do with what I saw."

"Mr. Small, I'm the Judge in this courtroom and I'll decide that. Now answer the question."

Inez became concerned about Galen's attitude. *Just answer the damn question,* she thought to herself.

Galen exhaled.

"Repeat the question." Judge VanCulver instructed Douglas.

"Mr. Small did you receive a verbal warning for encouraging the black children not to play with the white children? Yes or no?"

"Yeah, because. . . ."

Douglas interrupted. "I'm not interested in why, Mr. Small."

"But you need to know why. It's not just a yes or no answer. There's a reason."

Douglas turned to Judge VanCulver.

Judge VanCulver banged his gavel. "Mr. Small, answer the question either yes or no, and don't offer an explanation if you're not asked for one. Do you understand?"

"But, it's not fair that I don't get to explain myself."

Judge VanCulver removed his glasses. "Mr. Small, what did I just tell you?"

Douglas raised an eyebrow toward Inez. Apparently, it was his turn to gloat.

Inez shook her head at Joey.

"Continue, Mr. Pratt," Judge said.

"Isn't it true that it was Mr. Clayborn who gave you a verbal warning for trying to segregate the children?"

Galen stared at Douglas. "So."

Douglas again looked at Judge VanCulver.

The Judge said, "Mr. Small, please answer yes or no."

Galen frowned. "Yeah."

"Mr. Small, you don't like Robert Clayborn and you filed a grievance against him, not because he didn't give you the job, but because he gave the job to a white person. It is a known fact that you don't like white people. Isn't that the truth?"

Galen folded his arms and glared at Douglas. "You tell me, since you know so much."

Douglas sneered. "Me, tell you? All right, Mr. Small, I'll tell you."

Douglas went back to his table and grabbed some papers. He handed Inez a copy and then gave Galen a copy.

When Inez read through the papers, she dropped her head and passed them to Joey. Joey shook his head.

"Mr. Small, you were arrested for disturbing the peace five years ago. You used racial slurs during what was suppose to be a peace rally. You referred to white people as honkies, pecker woods, and rednecks, didn't you?"

"But what happened was...."

Douglas interrupted again. "Mr. Small, I'm not interested in the details. Answer the question, yes or no."

Galen pointed. "Look man, I told you before, it's not that simple. It's not a yes or no answer. There's more to it."

Douglas seemed to be having a ball with the bigot. "Your Honor, please instruct the witness again to answer yes or no."

Before Judge VanCulver could speak, Galen interrupted. "Instruct me? What do you mean?" Galen slapped his chest. "Talk to me," he said to Douglas, then pointed to Judge VanCulver, "not him."

Obviously upset with Galen, Judge VanCulver swiveled back and forth in his chair. He leaned over, fixed his gaze on Galen. "Mr. Small, I told you this is my courtroom and, like it or not, you'll do as I say. I'm in charge, Sir. I make the rules."

Galen leaned towards the Judge. "This ain't four hundred years ago. I ain't nobody's slave."

Judge VanCulver banged his gavel, pointed and growled at Galen. "One more remark like that and I'll have you held in contempt of court."

Police officers Edwards and Olson eyeballed Galen. Not sure of what the witness was capable of, they slowly moved towards Galen.

Inez shook her head and thought to herself, *No, you're not a slave, but you're sure an asshole.* Totally frustrated, she wondered what the hell Galen was doing. She wished he would shut up. She didn't even know how to object. She examined the jury and read discontent on their faces.

Maxwell Cane sat in the back row of the jury box and watched with clenched teeth. He looked as if he were ready to leap over the other jurors and attack Galen.

Inez knew his arrogance, ignorance and blatant dislike for the Caucasian race overshadowed her successful examination of Galen. The more Galen spoke, the angrier she became. She sank deeper and deeper in her chair. Inez glared at Joey and he hunched his shoulders, obviously he didn't know what to do either.

Judge VanCulver eyed Galen. "Now, you answer the question yes or no."

"Okay, no."

Douglas glanced at Robert, then at Galen. "Mr. Small, you hate Mr. Clayborn, don't you?"

"Hey, Man, how many times are you going to ask me that?"

Inez shook her head.

Douglas said, "Your Honor. . . "

Galen interrupted, "I think Mr. Clayborn's unfair."

Douglas smiled. "C'mon, Mr. Small. You don't like him because he married a white woman. You have been extremely vocal in the past about your disapproval of Mr. Clayborn's interracial marriage. You don't like that." Douglas yelled. "Do you?"

Inez jumped up. She had to object. The jury was already frustrated and Galen had to be silenced. "Your Honor, I object. Mr. Pratt is badgering the witness."

Galen leaned forward and frowned at Douglas. "Hell no, I don't like him and I'm not to crazy about you either." Jennifer smiled while Robert stared at Galen.

Inez motioned her hand at Galen for him to stop. She really wanted him to be quiet. "Your Honor, I objected. Please rule."

Galen looked at Mr. Clayborn and yelled, "I think he's a sell-out. He's a kiss-ass for marrying the enemy."

Indistinct roars rang throughout the courtroom.

Judge VanCulver wrapped his gavel and yelled, "Order in the court."

Inez couldn't believe him. This was the worst witness she ever had. All she wanted was for Douglas to finish so Galen could disappear forever. The sight of Galen made her sick.

Beverly held Martin's hand. Beverly didn't understand what exactly was going on, but unmistakably a predominantly white jury would not be happy with Galen's racist remarks.

Martin, on the other hand, with his experience in the courtroom, probably knew Galen's testimony hurt Inez's case immensely.

When the courtroom became quiet, Judge VanCulver spoke. "I'll not tolerate these outbursts. Another eruption and I'll clear this courtroom."

Judge VanCulver said, "Ms. Connors, your objection is overruled. Take your seat." It was obvious he was irritated at Galen's remarks. The Judge instructed Douglas to continue.

Douglas gawked at Galen. "Your racist attitude is what brought you here. It's not because of what you saw, but you knew it was your opportunity to get back at Robert Clayborn, or as you put it, this kiss-ass, for not giving you the head librarian position."

Galen didn't respond.

"I'm through with this man, Your Honor. I have no further questions."

"Redirect, Ms. Connors?"

Inez shook her head and spoke softly. "No, Your Honor." She turned toward the exit sign over the entrance of the courtroom, then at Galen. *Get your ass off the stand and* get *out of here*, she thought.

As Galen left the courtroom, he stopped at the plaintiff's table. "I tried to help, Ms. Connors. That's all I wanted to do."

Inez didn't respond. Galen left.

It was about two-fifteen and Inez prayed Judge VanCulver would adjourn until tomorrow.

The high winds whistled and the raindrops pounded against the floor to ceiling windows that surrounded the courtroom.

"Call your next witness, Ms. Connors." Judge instructed.

Inez stood slowly and called Jeffrey Garrison to the stand.

Mr. Garrison's examination would be short and simple. He knew nothing. He was needed to corroborate that he received statements and that he notified Beverly Monday.

Mr. Garrison stood tall and straight as he proceeded to take the witness stand.

"State your full name for the record."

"Jeffrey Garrison."

Inez sat down and remained in her seat. Galen's testimony had exhausted her. "What is your occupation, Mr. Garrison?"

"I'm president of the MTU for the Melbourne Public School System."

"Tell the jury what that stands for."

"MTU stands for Melbourne Teachers' Union."

"Mr. Garrison did you have occasion to talk to members of the union regarding this case?"

"Yes."

"Please tell the court the nature of those discussions."

"I received a visit from Ella Walker regarding another issue. During our conversation, Mrs. Walker reported that Jennifer Reinhart was displaying abusive behavior to one of the cognitively disabled students in her classroom."

"Who was that student?"

"Bryce Monday."

"What did you do?"

"I instructed her to report what she saw to the principal, Robert Clayborn."

"Did she?"

"Yes."

"What happened?"

"Mrs. Walker indicated she had talked to Mr. Clayborn about the abuse and Mr. Clayborn did nothing."

Inez didn't want to mention Galen Small's name again in front of the jury. "You received other statements about the abuse?"

"Yes. Initially I received phone calls from Agnes Harris and Galen Small."

"What about them? Did they speak to Mr. Clayborn?"

"Ms. Harris and Mr. Small said they didn't bother to speak to Mr. Clayborn because they both felt he wouldn't do anything."

"Why not?"

"I asked Ms. Harris and Mr. Small the same question and they both stated they felt because they had pending grievances against Mr. Clayborn, he would not do anything."

"Mr. Garrison, what happened next?"

"I asked all three of them to write down what they observed and submit it to me."

"What did you do then?"

"I called Bryce Monday's mother, Beverly Monday. I asked her to meet with me and she agreed. I showed her the three statements."

"What did Beverly Monday do?"

"Ms. Connors," Mr. Garrison swallowed hard, "that was the worse thing I've ever had to do." Mr. Garrison sighed and shook his head. "The look on that woman's face when she read the statements."

Beverly muzzled her mouth with her hand, tears streamed down her cheeks, she shook her head.

"I understand, Mr. Garrison. Please continue." Inez said.

"I gave her the statements and the poor woman nearly collapsed."

"Thank you, Mr. Garrison. No further questions."

"Cross-examine, Mr. Pratt?" Judge VanCulver asked.

Seated, Douglas crossed his legs and twirled his pen. "Mr. Garrison, did you attempt to talk to Mr. Clayborn regarding these allegations?"

"No."

"You just took it for granted that this alleged abuse took place and that Mr. Clayborn would not do anything based on what Ella Walker, Agnes Harris and Galen Small told you."

"They had no reason to lie, Sir."

"I just don't understand, Mr. Garrison, why you didn't at least give Mr. Clayborn a chance?"

Mr. Garrison didn't respond.

"You represent Agnes Harris, Galen Small and Ella Walker in their grievances against Mr. Clayborn, don't you?"

"Yes, I do."

"Knowing these three didn't exactly get along with Mr. Clayborn because of their grievances, it never dawned on you that, maybe, these accusations were unfounded?"

"Like I said, Sir, they had no reason to lie."

Douglas looked at the jury. "I think the court might differ, Mr. Garrison."

Inez jumped to her feet. "Your Honor, I object."

"Sustained. Jurors please disregard Mr. Pratt's last remark," the Judge instructed.

Douglas took his seat. "I have no further questions for this witness, Your Honor."

"Due to the late hour and the weather, now would be a good time to adjourn. Court will resume tomorrow at nine a.m." Judge VanCulver banged his gavel. Court was adjourned at three o'clock.

Mr. Evans yelled, "All rise."

The jury exited, Judge VanCulver followed.

CHAPTER TWENTY-THREE

Galen Small had damaged Inez's case. Douglas Pratt had conveniently diverted the jury's attention from the abuse to Galen's bigotry. Inez only had one witness left and that was Beverly Monday, the mother who was informed that her child had been abused but had not witnessed any maltreatment of her son.

The only chance Inez had was to somehow expose the truth during her cross-examination of the defendants.

The rain continued and the powerful winds trilled in the night. The thunder sounded like drums and lightning brightened the sky. There were power failures in sections of Melbourne and some damage to homes due to flying debris. It took Inez an additional half-hour to get home. A tree had blocked the exit ramp to Beaver Point and traffic was forced to detour.

When Inez arrived home, she showered and changed into her jungle green silk pajamas. She went to the refrigerator to get some juice when the doorbell rang.

When Inez opened the door, Joey stood on the porch drenched from head to toe. Inez grabbed his wrist and pulled him inside. "Oh, my God, Joey. What the hell are you doing out in this weather? You're soaked."

"I wanted to make sure you're okay."

"A phone call would have done it."

"I tried to call, but the storm has damaged the phone lines in your area."

Inez went to the bathroom closet and brought out a face towel and a beach towel. She patted Joey's head with the towel to soak up the water from his dark brown hair. She handed him the beach towel. "Remove your shirt and dry off. You're going to get pneumonia."

Joey removed his long sleeved white shirt. The water glistened as it dripped from his smooth mahogany chest.

His navy blue dress pants were dripping. "Go in the bathroom and take everything off. I can throw these wet clothes in the dryer. There's another beach towel in the closet you can wrap around you."

After Joey changed, he rejoined Inez in the living room. He handed her his wet clothes and she threw them in the dryer.

"You must be freezing." Inez said. "Would you like a warm drink? How about a cup of coffee, or maybe some tea or hot chocolate?"

"No, thanks."

Inez went to the refrigerator and poured herself a glass of cranberry juice and sat on the couch next to Joey. "I've never had a witness as terrible as Galen Small. Court was a disaster today." She sipped the juice.

"I know, but I think you still have a shot at winning this case."

"I don't know how. Beverly is my last witness. She didn't see anything. She can only testify that she's Bryce's mother and she came to me because she was informed her son had been abused."

"Don't worry about it, Inez. Regardless of the damage Galen caused, the fact remains Jennifer Reinhart was not qualified to teach those children."

"I can't lose this case. Fate brought Beverly to me. I'm the one chosen to obtain justice for Bryce. I have to do it for Bryce. That little boy is depending on me."

"Inez, don't take this case personal."

Inez nibbled her nail.

"Inez, do you hear me?"

"I hear you, Joey. You don't understand. I have to take it personally. I guess you can't understand because you don't have children."

Inez opened her briefcase and read through her questions for trial tomorrow.

Joey sat quietly.

About twenty minutes later, Joey cleared his throat, then stood. "You don't have to have children to know that abuse is wrong. Do you think my clothes are dry?"

Inez removed Joey's clothes from the dryer and he changed in the bathroom. Dressed, Joey returned to the living room where Inez stood in the middle of the room with her arms folded, apparently back in deep thought.

Joey headed towards the door. "Thanks for drying my clothes. I'll see you in court at nine in the morning."

Inez followed him to the door. "Joey, I'm sorry. I didn't mean to upset you."

"Don't worry about it." He smiled. "Get some sleep."

* * *

Martin rolled over in bed, Beverly was gone. He went to Bryce's room and he was asleep. He went to the living room and found Beverly curled in a fetal position on the couch. He sat next to her. "Baby, it's two o'clock in the morning. We've got to get up early. Come back to bed."

"I can't sleep." Beverly said.

"Don't worry about the trial. A setback doesn't necessarily mean a loss. You have to trust the system and Inez. A prayer would help to." He rubbed her back.

Beverly reached for the newspaper on the cocktail table. "Martin, did you read the paper today?"

"No."

Beverly turned to page five then handed the paper to Martin. "Read this."

Martin scanned the article. "Baby, this doesn't mean you won't win."

"Why not? The white teacher was acquitted of abusing a nine-year-old black girl in Michigan. This child testified as to what the teacher did to her and the teacher was still found not guilty. What chance do I have?"

"You can't base your situation on this without knowing the specifics of the case."

"You know, Martin, I remember about three years ago reading about a case in Maine where a black teacher was found guilty of abuse. The teacher was accused of abusing a twelve-year-old white boy. The boy claimed the teacher twisted his arm and pushed him in the back of his head. That woman was found guilty."

Martin ran his fingers through Beverly's hair. "You think because the teacher was black and the student was white is why there was a conviction, don't you?"

"It's sad to say, but yes, I do."

Martin stood. "C'mon, let's go to bed. We have to stay positive and whatever happens, win or lose, I'll be there for you. I'll never leave you again."

* * *

The weather bureau issued an all clear in Melbourne, Wisconsin at seven-thirty a.m.

CHAPTER TWENTY-FOUR

It was fifty-two degrees and cloudy. Branches and debris were scattered about Melbourne, but there were no injuries or serious damage.

Court began at nine-fifteen instead of nine. Judge VanCulver was delayed in traffic. When he entered the courtroom he apologized and instructed Inez to call her next witness.

"I call Beverly Monday." Inez said.

Beverly stood and walked to the stand. She rubbed her left forearm with her right hand, obviously nervous. Beverly glanced at the jury, then to Jennifer. She repeated the oath after Mr. Evans, brushed the skirt of her navy blue suit before sitting down. She kept her sweaty hands in her lap, out of the jury's eyesight, and twisted her fingers.

"State your name for the record," Inez said.

"Beverly Ann Monday."

"Where do you live?"

"Melbourne, Wisconsin."

"What is your address?"

"Eight Twenty-seven East Portland Boulevard."

"How long have you lived there?"

"For eight years."

"Where are you employed, Ms. Monday?"

"Bertram Group Insurance."

"For how long?"

"Ten years."

The foreman, Louis DeChambr, hid a yawn behind his hand. It was apparent to Inez the jurors were bored. She knew she'd better pick up the pace. After Galen's testimony yesterday, Inez had lost a lot of ground with the jury. Even Judge VanCulver's head was down. Others in the courtroom probably assumed he was reading, but being closer to him at the lectern, Inez could see that his eyes were closed.

"Do you have children, Ms. Monday?"

"Yes."

"How many?"

"One."

"What is your child's name?"

"His name is Bryce Monday."

"Tell us about your son."

Beverly swallowed hard. "Bryce is eight years old. When he was born, the doctors told me his brain didn't fully develop and because of this he would be cognitively disabled."

"Ms. Monday, tell us about Bryce's disabilities."

Beverly's voice slightly trembled. "Bryce can't dress himself. He's not potty-trained. I have to bathe him and he can't communicate. He can only say 'no' and 'mommy', but it's not real clear."

"Are you familiar with Bryce's teacher?"

Beverly dashed a view at Jennifer Reinhart. "Yes."

"What is her name?"

"Jennifer Reinhart."

"Did you communicate with Ms. Reinhart regularly about Bryce?"

"Yes. The first part of the year, I visited the school frequently because my mother passed away and I took a leave of absence from work."

"How often did you visit?"

"Three to four times a week."

"When did you return to work?"

"February this year."

It was silent throughout the courtroom. All eyes on Beverly.

"With Bryce's disabilities, was there any special care instructions that you discussed with Ms. Reinhart?"

"Yes."

"What?"

"The one thing I stressed to Ms. Reinhart at the beginning of the school year was that Bryce really loves milk but not from a cup."

"Would you explain that for the jury?"

Beverly looked at the jury and spoke softly. "I don't know why or even if it has anything to do with his disability, but for some reason Bryce won't drink milk if it's in a cup. I pour it over cereal and he's fine with that. He'll drink water, juice, even soda in a cup, but not milk."

"When you told Ms. Reinhart, what did she say?"

"She said it wasn't a problem."

"When did you last speak to Ms. Reinhart?"

"I believe it was the last day of school. She called me at work."

"What was the nature of her phone call?"

"She wanted to meet with me. She said she needed to talk to me about something."

"About what?"

"I don't know. I asked but she wouldn't say. She said she didn't want to talk about it on the phone. I asked if it was about Bryce and she said no."

"Ms. Reinhart gave you no clue as to why she wanted to meet with you?"

"The only thing she said was she might need me to defend her."

"In what way?"

"I don't know. We never met."

"What do you mean? Why didn't you meet?"

"I agreed to meet Ms. Reinhart at my home that evening, but when I got home, she called and said she would not be coming. She said she'd taken care of her problem."

"Ms. Monday, what happened next?"

Jennifer sat at attention and stared at Beverly. Douglas' lips lifted in a sarcastic grin.

"Later that night I received a phone call from Jeffrey Garrison. He asked me to come to his office. I did and he. . . ." Beverly began to breathe hard. She seemed unable to finish what she was saying.

"Ms. Monday, would you like some water?"

"Yes, please."

Mr. Evans left the courtroom and immediately returned with a cup of water for Beverly. Beverly's hand trembled as she gulped it down.

"Take your time, Ms. Monday." Inez said. "Can you continue?"

"Yes, thank you. When I went to Mr. Garrison's office he showed me statements from teachers that said they had seen Jennifer Reinhart abuse my son. I took the statements and gave them to you."

Inez glanced at the jury. "You testified earlier that because of Bryce's disabilities you have to bathe him." Beverly wiped her eyes.

"Yes, I do."

"Have you ever noticed any marks or bruises on Bryce's body while you were bathing him?"

"Yes, one night when I was bathing Bryce, I noticed a bruise on his back."

Inez wanted the jury to see the correlation between the bruise on Bryce's back and that Ella Walker and Galen Small testified that Jennifer put her knee in his back. Inez was not surprised that Douglas had not objected. Undoubtedly, because Beverly told what happened that led her to court. She didn't see anything. She was a mother searching for the truth.

"Ms. Monday, do you know how Bryce got the bruise?"

"No. I thought he probably fell because he trips over his feet a lot because his feet are turned in. Sometimes he loses his balance. Now I know he got it when Jennifer put her knee in his back."

Douglas immediately sprang to his feet and hollered, "I object. Purely speculation on the part of the witness."

"Sustained."

"Did you ever notice any other marks or bruises on Bryce?"

"He came home from school one day with a busted lip."

"Did you question that?"

"Yes. I asked Ms. Reinhart what happened."

"What did she say?"

Beverly sniffled. "She told me he fell."

"You heard Galen Small testify that around the end of May, beginning of June, he witnessed Bryce's lip bleeding as a result of Jennifer Reinhart forcing his face to the floor."

Beverly wiped her tears. "Yes."

"Ms. Monday, when did Bryce come home with a busted lip?"

"Around the end of May?"

Douglas instantly sprang to his feet. "Your Honor, I object. Ms. Connors is leading the witness."

Before Judge VanCulver could rule, Inez yelled, "I withdraw the question."

Inez felt she had gained some ground with the jury with Beverly's testimony. Enough of the jurors had children and would sympathize with Beverly. She was hopeful they would not hold Galen's fiasco against Beverly.

Judge VanCulver seemed mesmerized by a stain on the ceiling, probably a leak from the storm last night.

"One last question, Ms. Monday. Prior to the phone call from Jeffrey Garrison you had no knowledge of what was going on in the classroom, isn't that right?"

Beverly brushed her teary eyes. "Not an inkling."

"No further questions." Inez sat down.

"Your witness, Mr. Pratt." Judge VanCulver said.

Inez smiled as Douglas unbuttoned his suit coat as if he was ready to do battle with the distraught mother. Inez was confident Douglas would tread lightly with Beverly because he didn't want the fragile woman to breakdown in front of the jury.

Douglas strode up to the lectern.

"Ms. Monday, my name is Douglas Pratt and I understand your concern. I'm a parent and I would want to get to the truth regarding accusations about my child."

Beverly nodded as if to say, "Thank you."

Douglas began his attack. "Ms. Monday, do you love your son?"

Beverly raised her eyebrows. "Of course, I do."

"Have you ever been in trouble with the law?"

"No."

"What is your marital status?"

"Single."

"You've never been married, not even to Bryce's father?"

"No. We were never married."

Martin leaned forward and whispered to Inez. "What the hell is he up to?"

Inez shrugged and looked at Joey. Joey didn't know either.

"Ms. Monday, have you ever abused Bryce?" Douglas asked.

Inez immediately jumped to her feet. "I object, Your Honor. My client is not the one on trial."

Before Judge VanCulver could rule, Douglas yelled, "Isn't it a fact that six years ago your son's father, Willie Flinn, accused you of abusing your illegitimate son?"

Murmurs bubbled throughout the courtroom.

Inez glanced at Beverly. "Don't say a word." Inez looked at Judge VanCulver. "Your Honor, Mr. Pratt is out of order. He has not allowed you to rule before he asked another question."

Judge VanCulver banged his gavel until the courtroom was quiet. "Both counselors approach the bench." Judge VanCulver said sternly.

Beverly and Martin exchanged glares. She was in tears, and it was apparent that Martin wanted to go to her and comfort her. Martin smiled and he lifted his chin with his finger, his way of telling her to keep her chin up.

The jurors appeared shocked. Some frowned, others mouths hung open.

Beverly was supposed to recapture their hearts, but it was obvious Douglas was attempting to destroy any belief the jurors had in her.

Judge VanCulver spoke softly but enunciated in an exaggerated fashion. "Mr. Pratt, you've been practicing law long enough to know better. Don't make the mistake of trying that again in my court. Ms. Connors, I'm going to allow Mr. Pratt to continue."

Inez frowned. "But, Your Honor. . . ."

Judge VanCulver interrupted and squinted at her, "Ms. Connors, don't say a word, just take your seat." Judge peered at Beverly, then said, "Answer the question, Ma'am."

Inez sat down and shook her head. Douglas had to be fishing. Beverly never mentioned Bryce's father had accused her of child abuse. Inez stared at Beverly and sensed there was some validity to Douglas' accusation.

Douglas moved back to the lectern.

"Ms. Monday, I'll repeat the question. Isn't it a fact Bryce's father, Willie Flinn, reported to the authorities that you abused your son?"

Beverly scooted to the edge of her chair. Her voice trembled, in tears. She cried, "But I can explain."

"Ms. Monday, please answer yes or no. Did you or did you not appear in family court six years ago because Willie Flinn, Bryce's father, accused you of abusing your own son?"

Inez's pen fell from her hand. She watched the pen roll across the table and drop to the floor. Inez did not understand why Beverly never mentioned something as important as this to her.

Beverly looked at Inez for help. The Judge had already ruled, Beverly had to answer.

Beverly said, "Yes!" She buried her face in her hands and cried.

Douglas approached the witness box. "Ms. Monday, you've brought charges against this woman," he pointed to Jennifer, "for abuse, and the reality is that you're the abuser."

Tears streamed down Beverly's face. "I didn't abuse my child. I would never hurt my baby. Willie is a liar."

"Ms. Monday, you just admitted that you appeared in family court for abuse. Your son's father," he paused. "Never mind. I think we've all heard enough." He looked at the jury. "I have no further questions."

Beverly stood and screamed at Douglas. "Willie's a liar. I did not abuse my son and he's not my son's father. Why won't you let me explain?"

The volume of noise ignited in the courtroom. Beverly cried uncontrollably.

Every juror in the jury box frowned at Beverly.

Inez leaned forward, stared at Beverly and shook her head. Judge VanCulver banged his gavel unsuccessfully. The voices in the courtroom escalated.

Jennifer grinned and showed her teeth for the first time.

Douglas was elated. It was obvious he had no idea Willie wasn't Bryce's father. Inez didn't know it either.

Gibber-jabber reeked throughout the courtroom. Candace, the court reporter, stopped typing. She could not decipher Beverly's words. Beverly was out of control.

Beverly screamed. "I didn't abuse my baby, Jennifer Reinhart did. I swear to God, that's the truth."

Judge finally ordered the courtroom cleared except for counsels and defendants.

Officers, Edwards and Olson, immediately escorted the spectators out of the courtroom. Beverly finally regained her composure and Judge VanCulver asked Inez if she wanted to redirect. Inez shook her head and softly said, "No, Your Honor."

Judge advised Beverly to step down and return to her seat.

He adjourned for the day.

CHAPTER TWENTY-FIVE

Martin left the premises when Judge VanCulver ordered the courtroom cleared. He didn't bother to wait for Beverly.

Inez left the courtroom upset. She never said a word to Beverly or Joey.

Joey ended up giving Beverly a ride home. They exchanged only a few words before Joey parked in front of Beverly's house.

Beverly looked over at Joey. Her eyes were pink from crying. "I don't know what happened to Martin. Inez is mad at me. Isn't she?"

"Wouldn't you be mad, Beverly? Why didn't you tell her?"

"I didn't think it would come up."

Joey shook his head. "You still should've told her."

Beverly said softly, "I realize that now."

"I've never seen her work this hard on a case. It's like Bryce is her child. I think she's hurt more than anything."

Beverly opened the car door.

Joey sighed. "Be strong. It's not the end of the world."

Beverly closed the door and went inside. She plopped down on the couch and decided to call Sharon.

"Sharon, it's me. You can bring Bryce home tonight, and I'll drop him off on my way to court in the morning?"

"He's asleep, let him stay. You know I took time off to be with Bryce while you're in court."

"Oh, I forgot."

"Beverly, what's going on? Martin was here for a few minutes and he said you broke down on the witness stand and the Judge had to clear the courtroom."

"That damn Willie told Attorney Pratt about the child abuse charges he filed against me."

"Beverly, why in the hell didn't you tell Ms. Connors and especially Martin about the abuse charges?"

"I didn't think I needed to."

"Did you explain?"

"No, they wouldn't let me."

"Bev, once you explain, Ms. Connors will understand. Girl, when Martin came over, he looked terrible. He seemed really hurt and angry. He hugged Bryce so tight I thought he was going to squeeze the life out of the child. You need to talk to him."

"What else did Martin tell you, Sharon?"

"That's basically it. He kissed Bryce, told him he loved him and left. Although I had the feeling there was more, I didn't question him. Is there?"

Beverly started to cry.

"Beverly, what is it? What else happened?"

Before Beverly could answer, the doorbell rang.

"Sharon, I'll call you back. That's probably Martin. I'll explain everything later." Beverly hung up. She quickly wiped her tears and opened the door. It was Inez.

Inez entered and stood in the middle of the living room.

"Have a seat." Beverly said.

"Oh, cut it out, Beverly. Why in the hell didn't you tell me about the abuse charges?"

"I didn't think it would come up."

"You still should've told me. I can't believe it. You never said a damn word."

"How was I supposed to know that Willie was going to contact Mr. Pratt? I thought his threat was idle."

Wrinkles crimped Inez's forehead. "He threatened you?"

"Yes, but I never heard from him again. I figured he was bluffing."

Inez crossed her arms. "You should've let me decide about that." Inez collapsed on the couch. "Do you want to tell me what happened? Why did Willie have you brought up on charges of child abuse?"

Beverly started to pace. "About six years ago, when Willie and I was still together, we had a fight. I can't even remember what it was about. Bryce was crying and I picked him up and screamed, I wish you would be quiet. I held him up in the air. I didn't shake him or do anything to hurt him. The next thing I knew Willie took Bryce to Melbourne General Hospital and said I shook him. The attending physician called the police. I was subpoenaed to family court and when the judge heard my side of the story, he dropped the charges. The judge felt it was a misunderstanding between me and Willie. He said Willie used Bryce to get even with me. There was never any record of this. The judge dismissed all charges against me. Willie had to have told Mr. Pratt about this. It's the only way he could have found out."

"If that's the case, why would Willie do that?"

"Willie called me when he heard about the lawsuit. I hadn't heard from him in years. He told me that if I won, he wanted half of the settlement. I refused. He told me if I didn't agree he would tell. I thought the asshole was joking. I never heard from him again, so I assumed he was bluffing. That's why I never said anything." Beverly started to cry. "I swear to God, I'm telling you the truth."

"Don't you see, if you had told me, I could have mentioned it when I questioned you. We could have put the truth out before Pratt the Prick misconstrued everything in the jury's mind. Then you blurt out that Willie is not Bryce's father."

"That's not what I meant. I'm sorry. I was mad at Willie."

"Is Willie Bryce's father?" Inez asked.

"Yes, biologically, but if he was a real father to Bryce, he wouldn't try to use his son for capital gain. That's what I meant." Beverly cleared her throat. "Put me back on the stand so I can explain what really happened."

"And give Pratt another shot at you? I can't do that."

"Please, Inez. Joey said we still have a chance."

Inez jumped up. "I can't continue with this case. I have to withdraw."

Beverly grabbed Inez by both arms and yelled. "Please, you can't do that. I need you. You can't let them get away with this."

Inez pulled out of Beverly's grasp and headed towards the door. "When you came to me, I honestly thought you wanted my help. I can't fight them and you to."

"It's easy for you. You don't have children. You have no idea how I feel." Beverly said.

Inez stopped immediately and spun around. She squinted at Beverly and clenched her fist. "How dare you. You have no idea what you're talking about. My child was killed at the hands of a drunk driver. So don't you tell me I don't know how it feels. I know better than you. I'm sure you were devastated when you were told Bryce was abused. I was told my child was dead."

"I'm sorry, Inez. I didn't know."

Inez pointed her finger at Beverly. "Don't you ever fucking tell me I don't know how you feel. No, lady, you don't know how I feel." Inez cried as she made her way to the door.

Beverly circled Inez's wrist. "Inez, please, I'm so sorry. I know you care. Don't abandon me. Bryce doesn't have a chance without you. Please don't punish him for what I've done."

Inez slammed the door behind her.

Beverly plopped down on the couch. She called Martin at home and at the office but couldn't reach him. She cried herself to sleep.

* * *

Inez went back to the office. She fought her way through the protestors and found Joey hard at work.

"I thought everybody had gone. What are you doing?" She asked.

"After I gave Beverly a ride home, I thought I'd come back to the office and look over our questions for the defendants." Inez dropped her briefcase on her desk and sank into her chair. "Don't bother. I just left Beverly and I told her I quit."

"Yeah, well you can just call her and tell her you've changed your mind. I'm not letting you go out like this."

Inez put her head down on the desk and started to cry again. "I'm sorry, Allie."

Joey went around the desk and pulled her up by her shoulders. "Inez, what do you mean, I'm sorry, Allie?"

"It's my fault Allie's dead. It really is."

"What are you talking about? You told me a drunk driver killed your daughter. How did she die?"

"I willed it."

Joey stood Inez to her feet. Her body was like a wet noodle as she cried.

"What do you mean you, willed it?"

"Joey, my little girl, was born cognitively disabled and for a second I wished she'd never been born. God took her." She cried hard and Joey hugged her tightly and stroked the back of her head.

"Sh-sh, don't cry. No wonder you take this case so personally. You feel like you've been given a second chance."

Inez cried harder. "Bryce is Allie and Allie is Bryce."

"Inez, if you really feel that way, that's all the more reason why you can't quit. Do it for Allie. Do it for Bryce. Win or lose."

* * *

Beverly was awakened at midnight by a knock on her door. Startled, at the continuous banging, she jumped up. As Beverly headed towards the door, she wondered, why, whoever it was, didn't ring the doorbell.

She opened the door. It was Martin. He looked terrible. His clothes were wrinkled, his shirt was partially tucked in his pants. His hair needed to be brushed. His eyes were bloodshot.

"Oh my God, Martin."

Martin didn't respond. He brushed past Beverly into the living room.

"Martin, I'm so upset. Just hold me." Beverly started towards Martin and he put up both hands.

"Don't touch me." Martin said.

"Martin, I can explain about the abuse."

"I don't give a damn about the abuse. I know that's a lie. You're not that kind of a person."

"Oh Martin."

Beverly started towards him again, but Martin backed up a couple of steps. "Beverly, he's my son, isn't he? Bryce is my son."

Beverly stopped, but didn't respond. She stared at Martin.

Martin yelled, "Answer me, dammit. He's my son, isn't he?"

"Martin, I can explain."

"I don't want your fucking explanations." He pointed. "You tell me and you tell me now, goddammit. Is Bryce my son?"

Beverly screamed. "Yes, he's your son."

Martin paced from one end of the couch to the other end. He stared at Beverly, hit the couch with his fist, and headed towards the door.

Beverly ran and threw herself in front of the door. "Martin, wait a minute. Please let me explain."

"Get out of my way," he yelled.

"I did it because I love you."

"You love me?" Martin screamed.

Beverly started to cry. "I couldn't tell you. Your mother was sick. She needed you more than I did. If I had told you, what would you have done?"

Martin didn't respond.

Beverly wiped her eyes. "You would've left and come back to Melbourne. Martin, you would've never forgiven me if you had not been at your mother's bedside when she died."

"When I met Willie, I was six weeks pregnant. We became intimate shortly after we met, so I let him believe Bryce was his son."

Martin started to cry. "All these years I had a son and you never said a word."

"Your mother was. . . ."

Martin interrupted. He slapped his chest and yelled. "You should've told me. It was my decision, my choice to make, not yours, and you took that choice away from me. He's my son. Bryce is my son," he yelled.

"I'm sorry. I did it because I love you."

"Shut up, Beverly. I don't want to hear it."

Martin wiped the tears from his face and inhaled through his nose. He looked at Beverly and shook his head. "For eight years I've had a son. I should've known he was my son. The first time I saw him, I fell in love with him. I felt something that I've never felt with another child. I felt connected to him. I thought it was because of my love for you."

Beverly yelled. "You left me, Martin. You left me and you never came back."

Martin reached around her and opened the door even as she leaned against it, forcing her to move. "So you punish me by keeping my son from me?" He stepped out into the hallway.

"Martin, I love you."

Martin turned around. "Why didn't you tell me after my mother died?"

"By then, you'd landed a job with the biggest law firm in Florida and I'd already met Willie. He assumed Bryce was his and I didn't tell him anything different."

"You got involved with an alcohol and drug abuser. You immediately fuck him so you can trick him into believing he's Bryce's father, and you say you love me?"

Beverly slapped Martin. "I'm not a slut. It didn't happen like that. Oh, Martin, I'm sorry. I didn't mean to hurt you."

Quietly, Martin said, "It didn't hurt. I didn't feel a thing." Tears slid down Martin's face. "Not telling me I had a son is what hurt."

"Martin, I'm sorry. I honestly thought I was doing the right thing."

"Right thing for you, but not for me."

"I love you, Martin. I have never stopped loving you. Please forgive me." Beverly pleaded.

"Why haven't you told me since we've been back together? Huh? Why haven't you?"

"Martin, please come inside and let's talk. I feel lousy."

"I agree Beverly, you are lousy."

"Martin, I love you. I'm sorry."

Martin wiped the tears from his face. His voice quivered. "You say you love me? Well I hate you. You say you're sorry?" He inhaled and added calmly, "Yeah, me too." He turned and strode away.

Beverly screamed after him, "Martin."

He never turned around.

* * *

Joey called Beverly later that night and informed her Inez would remain on the case.

CHAPTER TWENTY-SIX

Beverly arrived moments before trial began. Martin wasn't in court. Beverly kept glaring over her shoulder hoping that he would show up.

Inez smiled at Beverly and Beverly returned it.

When Judge VanCulver entered he looked at Inez. "Call your next witness, Ms. Connors."

"I rest my case, Your Honor."

"Very well. Mr. Pratt, call your first witness."

Douglas stood. "I call Vaughn Guftason to the stand."

Inez was not the least bit worried about Vaughn Guftason. His testimony would only corroborate Dr. Thrasher's: Bryce Monday was a cognitively disabled child with a mental capacity of an infant.

Vaughn Guftason was a nimble, tiny man. He spoke with a German accent and was well-dressed in a black wool suit.

"State your full name." Douglas said.

"Vaughn Guftason."

"What is your occupation?"

"I'm a child psychologist."

"Where did you receive your formal training, Dr. Guftason?"

"I received my degree at the University of Meridian in Meridian, North Carolina."

"How long have you been a doctor?"

"Twenty-five years."

Douglas paced from one end of the jury box to the other then back to the witness. "Doctor, you had occasion to visit with Bryce Monday at your office?"

"Yes I did."

"Tell us your professional opinion of Bryce."

Dr. Guftason removed the notebook from the inside pocket of his lapel. "I saw Bryce Monday once at my office. Bryce is microencephalic. Microencephaly is an abnormally small head caused by malformation of the brain. This condition causes developmental delays in children. Bryce is extremely small for his age. As part of my evaluation, I weighed Bryce. He weighed twenty-six pounds and he's three feet tall."

Everyone in the courtroom appeared bored. The fat, middle-aged juror rolled her eyes. The bald juror twiddled his thumbs and sighed. The only person who seemed to be paying attention to Dr. Guftason was Douglas. Dr. Guftason echoed Dr. Thrasher. No one doubted his credentials or his opinion about Bryce. Douglas wanted everyone in the courtroom to know that his expert witness was just as qualified as Inez's.

"Dr. Guftason, what is your medical opinion of Bryce Monday?" Douglas asked.

"I found the child to be mentally and physically delayed. He's ninety-nine percent nonverbal. My prognosis is that he will not advance much more mentally than he already has. I took x-rays of his brain and the left side is totally mal-formed."

"Thank you, Doctor. No further questions."

Judge VanCulver yawned. "Your witness, Counselor."

Inez remained seated. "Just a couple of questions, Doctor."

Dr. Guftason nodded.

"When you saw Bryce did he have a tantrum?"

"No."

"Did he try to bite you?"

"No, Ma'am."

"Did he display any type of behavior that would require you to restrain him."

"No, he did not."

"Thank you, Dr. Guftason. No further questions."

Judge VanCulver instructed Dr. Guftason to step down and instructed Attorney Pratt to call his next witness.

"I call Mora Abernathy to the stand."

Mora gracefully glided up to the witness stand. She wore a brown, double-breasted suit with a skirt. The suit was more conservative than usual, undoubtedly, at the advice of Douglas Pratt.

After Mora was sworn in, she fluffed her blonde hair, sat down and crossed her legs.

Douglas approached the lectern. "State your full name, please."

"Mora Marie Abernathy."

"Where are you employed, Ms. Abnerathy?"

"Melbourne Public School System."

"What is your occupation?"

"I'm Director of Special Education."

"How long have you held that title?"

"Eleven years."

"What does your position as director entail?"

"I hire and supervise teachers in the exceptional education classrooms. I'm assigned five elementary schools. I'm also responsible for monitoring the teachers on a monthly basis."

"What five elementary schools do you supervise?"

"Dane Elementary, Handelman Elementary, Carter Elementary, Fifth Street Elementary and Pleasant Grove Elementary."

"Do the teachers in these classrooms report directly to you?"

"Yes."

"Any other direct reports?"

"Yes, the principals at each school that I supervise also report directly to me."

"So Jennifer Reinhart and Robert Clayborn report to you?"

"Correct."

"What other responsibilities does your job involve?"

"I also assist in preparing the I.E.P. for each student in these classrooms."

"Explain to the jury what an I.E.P. is."

Mora looked at the jury. "An I.E.P. stands for Individualized Education Program. The school board appoints a staff to develop an individual education program for each child in a special education classroom. The staff is called the Multi-disciplinary Team, most often referred to as the M-Team. Each child's program is reviewed annually. Every child that receives special education is re-evaluated by an M-team every three years."

"Why, Ms. Abernathy?"

"To determine if the child should continue to receive special education."

Inez looked at the jury members and their attention was fading fast. The thin juror twirled his long gray beard. Judge VanCulver's eyelids drooped.

Douglas continued. "Ms. Abernathy, you keep using the term special education. Explain to the jury, briefly, what special education means."

Mora uncrossed her legs and looked at the jury. "Special education means specially designed teaching, free of charge, to the child and the child's parent to meet the extraordinary needs of a child with exceptional educational needs. That could include instruction in physical education and instruction conducted in the classroom or at home."

"Ms. Abernathy, please explain for us exceptional education."

"Exceptional Education, often referred to as Ex-Ed, is any child with special conditions, as determined by the state superintendent, who may require educational services to supplement or replace regular education."

"What are these special conditions, Ms. Abernathy?"

"Cognitive disability or other developmental disability, autism, learning disability, traumatic brain injury, visual handicap, hearing handicap, speech or language handicap, orthopedic impairment and emotional disturbance."

"What category does Bryce Monday fall into?"

"Bryce falls into the category of cognitive disability."

Inez was impressed. She wondered if Ms. Abernathy was really intelligent or if she did some serious studying before the trial. Probably the latter.

"Did you hire Jennifer Reinhart?"

"Yes, I did."

"Was she qualified?"

"Yes. I would not have hired Ms. Reinhart if she weren't."

"Ms. Abernathy, were you ever notified of the allegations against Jennifer Reinhart?"

"No."

"Did Robert Clayborn ever come to you about anything concerning Ms. Reinhart's treatment of Bryce Monday?"

"No. Never."

"When did you initially find out about the allegations being made by Ella Walker, Galen Small and Agnes Harris against Ms. Reinhart?"

"When Melbourne Public School System was served with court papers filed by Attorney Connors on behalf of Beverly Monday."

"Ms. Abernathy, is Jennifer Reinhart still employed by Melbourne Public School System?"

"Ms. Reinhart has been suspended with pay, pending the outcome of the trial."

Beverly glanced at Joey, then Inez. She grabbed Joey's notepad and wrote: *Jennifer Reinhart was suspended with pay? That's like being on a paid vacation.*

"No further questions." Douglas sat down.

"Ms. Connors, your witness." Judge VanCulver said.

Inez approached the witness with a file folder. "Ms. Abernathy, you said that you hire and supervise the teachers in these special education classrooms."

"Yes, that's correct."

"What are the main qualifications a person must possess to teach a child like Bryce Monday?"

"Bryce is cognitively disabled."

"That's not my question, Ms. Abernathy. My question is, what are the main qualifications an individual must possess in order to teach a child like Bryce Monday?"

"You need a Bachelor's Degree in education."

"Just education? Shouldn't it be specialized in some fashion?"

"No."

Inez's brow shot upward. "No?"

"No."

Inez opened her file and flipped through her notes.

Inez handed Mora a piece of paper. "Ms. Abernathy, here's a copy of the Wisconsin State Statutes with regard to children with exceptional education needs." Inez handed Douglas and Judge VanCulver a copy.

Inez approached Mora. "It clearly states in Subchapter V that the State of Wisconsin requires a teacher of severely cognitively disabled children to have not only a Bachelor's Degree, but a minimum of a Master's Degree in order to obtain a teaching credential. Not only that, Ms. Abernathy, in addition to obtaining a Master's Degree, a teacher must also complete an eighteen-week teacher training program before they can become licensed."

Douglas couldn't object to a state statute, not without making a fool of himself.

"Did Jennifer Reinhart have a Master's Degree when you interviewed her?"

"No."

"What did she have?"

"Like I said, it was a Bachelor's Degree."

Inez stared at the jury. "So it would be safe to conclude that since Ms. Reinhart didn't have a Master's Degree, she never completed the eighteen-week teacher training program. Correct?"

Mora didn't respond. Inez turned her ear towards her.

"Excuse me, I didn't hear you."

"That's true."

"So Ms. Reinhart's not licensed?"

Calmly Mora said. "Ms. Reinhart has a Bachelor's Degree in education. We sometimes place teachers in these classrooms when we're short-staffed."

Inez again looked at the jury. "You sometimes place unqualified teachers in severely disabled classrooms because you're short-staffed?"

"Objection, Your Honor," Mr. Pratt yelled from his seat.

"Overruled."

Sarcastically Inez said to Mora, "You have to answer the question."

Ms. Abernathy squirmed in her seat. "Ms. Reinhart is a qualified teacher."

Jennifer smiled.

"You stated earlier that one of your duties is to supervise the teachers who report to you?'

"Yes."

"How do you do that?"

"I make unannounced visits to the classroom to observe."

"How many times in a school year do you make these classroom visits?"

"Sometimes twice a month, sometimes less. It all depends on my schedule."

"How many times did you visit Jennifer Reinhart's classroom."

Mora paused. "I never visited her classroom."

Inez frowned, and gazed at the jury as if to convey, "Can you believe this?"

"Ms. Abernathy, You hired an unqualified teacher, then you never monitored her?"

Judge VanCulver interrupted. "Ms. Connors, do you anticipate a lengthy cross-examination of this witness?"

Judge VanCulver was tired and Inez knew it. Inez had already established to the jury Ms. Abernathy hired Ms. Reinhart knowing that she was not qualified. She didn't want to irritate the jury or the judge.

"Only a couple more questions, Your Honor."

Judge VanCulver exhaled. "Very well, continue."

"Ms. Abernathy, you said the principals at the five schools you supervise also report directly to you. Correct?"

"Yes."

"Do you visit the principals?"

"Yes."

"How often?'

"About once a month?"

"During the past school year, did you visit Robert Clayborn?"

"Yes."

"How many times?"

"Oh, I would say about three, maybe four times."

"So even when you visited the principal at Carter you never even bothered to stop in to check on Jennifer Reinhart?"

"Ma'am, I'm on a tight schedule."

"Where is the principal's office at Carter Elementary?"

"It's on the first floor."

"Where's Ms. Reinhart's classroom?"

"On the second floor."

"You could visit the principal, but your tight schedule wouldn't permit you to stop in and check on a teacher that you hired who lacked qualifications?"

Mora sprang forward. Apparently she'd had enough. "I told you. . . ."

Inez interrupted with, "No further questions. You may step down."

Immediately Douglas stood. "Your Honor, that was not necessary."

Judge VanCulver observed Inez. "Ms. Connors, you know better. I'll not tolerate that in my court."

"Sorry, Sir."

Judge VanCulver banged his gavel at three o'clock. "Court is adjourned until nine a.m. tomorrow."

* * *

Martin never appeared in court.

CHAPTER TWENTY-SEVEN

Inez went to the office after court. She fought her way through the anti-abortionists. She noticed three of the protestors hovering around a couple, apparently trying to convince them not to enter the clinic.

When she finally made it to her office, Inez sat at her desk paging through a law book. Inez closed it and threw it across the room. The case was nearing the end and she was behind in points with the jury. Galen's testimony and Beverly's outburst hurt tremendously.

Joey entered the office with coffee and cheeseburgers.

"How's it going?" he asked.

"I think I'm going to lose this one, Joey."

He handed her a cup of coffee and a cheeseburger.

Inez reached for the cream then put it down. "I'd better drink it black," she said. "I have a long night ahead of me."

"We both do."

They sipped their coffee and ate.

"What am I missing, Joey? Somebody's lying and if I don't figure it out, I'm going to lose and that bitch will be back in the system around children. The next child might not be as fortunate as Bryce."

Joey took a bite of his burger. "I wish you could put Beverly back on the stand so she could explain to the jury about the abuse charges filed against her."

"If I do that, Pratt will get another shot at her and he'll rip her apart. It would do more damage than good. She blurted out that Willie's not Bryce's father. Pratt will play that up to the jury. He'll have Beverly looking like a tramp just trying to make a buck."

Joey sipped his coffee. "You tell the jury what the circumstances were about the abuse charges."

"Me? How can I?"

"In your closing statement you can somehow let the jury know Beverly was falsely accused and the judge dismissed the charges."

"You know Pratt will object so loud, he'll have a heart attack." Inez bit her burger.

"Let him. And if Judge VanCulver instructs the jury to disregard what they heard, so be it. You know when something's been said it's hard for the jury to really forget."

Suddenly, there was a loud commotion outside. Inez and Joey ran to the window and looked out. Police cars and three police vans were parked in front of the building. The protestors had occupied the hallway leading to the clinic refusing to let anyone in. Apparently, the clinic called the police.

The officers stood in front of their vehicles and made no attempt to stop the protestors. Hopefully, their presence would be enough to maintain order.

"I knew there was going to be trouble today." Inez said to Joey. The protestors stopped a couple from entering the clinic when I came in."

"When I arrived I had the same feeling." Joey said.

Inez's phone rang. "Hi, Beverly. How's it going?"

"Okay. Have you seen Martin today? Is he at the office?"

"No, Beverly, I'm sorry, I haven't seen him in a couple days. Maybe, he's at home."

"I tried, no answer. Thanks." Beverly hung up.

"That was Beverly looking for Martin. She didn't even ask about the case."

"I'm sure he'll surface." Joey said. "He's hurt and people deal with hurt and anger differently. When he comes to grips with what happened, he'll talk to her."

"Are you sure about that?" Inez said.

"Of course, I'm sure."

"You know, Joey, Bryce resembles Martin. They both have curly hair. Beverly told me he's not the father. I do wonder."

Joey smiled. "Listen to yourself."

Inez smiled. "Well."

"Let's get back to the case." Joey said.

* * *

Sharon knocked at Beverly's door.

"Sharon, where's Bryce?"

"I left him with Tyler." Sharon came in and sat on the couch.

"I want to thank you, Sharon, for looking out for Bryce while the trial is going on."

"You know I don't mind it at all. Besides, I needed to take some time off anyway."

Beverly sat next to Sharon. "What do you mean it's nothing? You took time off to take care of him. I'm in trial all day and you go to check on him at school. That's a lot and I really do appreciate it."

"Beverly, did you talk to Martin?"

"Yes."

"And."

"He hates me. He stormed out of here and I haven't seen him since."

"Did you explain to him about the abuse charges?"

"Yes."

"I don't understand, Bev. He knows the court dismissed it because he felt Willie was using Bryce to get back at you because you were arguing. Being an attorney, Martin should know better."

Beverly's eyes filled with tears. She looked away trying to hide them from Sharon.

"That's not why he's mad." Beverly said.

Sharon gently turned Beverly's face towards her. "What else happened?"

"Sharon, Martin is Bryce's father."

Sharon jumped up. "What!"

"I blurted it out in court that Willie was not Bryce's father and Martin put two-and-two together." Beverly burst into tears and Sharon sat down and put her arms around her. "Sharon, he was so mad when he came by the house."

"Beverly, why didn't you tell him? That's why he looked so terrible."

"I told Martin I couldn't. His mother was sick and I didn't want him to come home because I was pregnant. After his mother died and Bryce was born, he was already established at the biggest law firm in Florida and I couldn't tell him then. I honestly thought I was doing the right thing." She cried.

Sharon hugged her sister tighter. "Why didn't you tell me?"

"I didn't want you involved. You already hated Willie and I didn't want you to lose your temper and say something to him about Martin."

Sharon released her embrace and wiped Beverly's tears. "Martin will be back. He loves you and Bryce."

"I've never seen him like this, Sharon. The way he looked at me, I think I've lost him for good this time. He'll never forgive me for not telling him he had a son."

* * *

After three hours, when ordered by the police, the protestors left the hallway leading to the clinic peacefully. There were no arrests.

CHAPTER TWENTY-EIGHT

The trial was nearing the end. As far as Inez could tell, Douglas Pratt had two witnesses left, Robert Clayborn and Jennifer Reinhart.

Susan Clayborn was in court again this morning, undoubtedly, to support her husband who would be testifying either today or tomorrow. Susan sat in the same seat, second row, first seat. Mora sat next to Susan.

Beverly looked around the courtroom and still no Martin. She thought Martin would, at least, put his anger aside to attend his son's case.

Judge VanCulver instructed Douglas to call his next witness.

Douglas stood and brushed the sleeves of his black suit. "I call Mr. Robert Clayborn to the stand."

Robert Clayborn hesitated momentarily, walked to the witness stand to be sworn in. His charcoal black hand vibrated as he raised it to be sworn in. He rubbed the few strands of hair on his balding head, and situated his bifocals on his face. He looked at Susan and she smiled at her obviously nervous husband.

Douglas walked up to the lectern. "Please state your full name for the record."

"Robert Farmer Clayborn."

"Where do you reside, Mr. Clayborn?"

"Lake Hills, Wisconsin."

"And your marital status?"

Robert glanced at Susan and smiled. "Married."

Susan returned a smile.

"Mr. Clayborn, is your wife here in court today?"

"Yes, she is."

"Where?"

Robert pointed. "That's her in the red and black dress."

Inez turned towards Joey and shook her head. She knew Douglas wanted the jury to see that Robert Clayborn's wife was a white woman, even though it was discussed in previous testimony, seeing was believing.

"Mr. Clayborn, how long have you been married?"

Inez stood. "Your Honor, I object. I fail to see the relevance of this line of questioning?"

"Sustained."

"Where are you employed, Mr. Clayborn"?

"I'm employed by Melbourne Public School System in Melbourne, Wisconsin."

"At which school?"

"Carter Elementary."

"In what capacity?"

Judge VanCulver's eyes were slightly closed.

"I'm the principal."

"Do you know Bryce Monday?"

"Yes, I do."

"How do you know him?"

"Bryce was a student at Carter Elementary in the cognitively disabled classroom."

"Do you know Galen Small?"

"Yes."

"Do you know Agnes Harris?"

"Yes I do."

"Do you know Ella Walker?"

"Yes."

"How do you know these people?"

"Galen Small is the assistant librarian at Carter. Ella Walker is a handicapped children's assistant and Agnes Harris teaches third grade at Carter."

"Have you ever had a confrontation with any of these employees at Carter Elementary?"

"Yes, I have."

"Tell the jury about it."

Robert cleared his throat and fixed his gaze at the jury. "Galen Small and Agnes Harris filed reverse discrimination grievances against me with the Melbourne Teacher's Union."

"And what about Ella Walker?"

"Mrs. Walker filed a grievance against me, claiming her six month performance review was unfair."

Douglas went back to his table and grabbed a folder then returned to the lectern. He flipped through the papers. "Mr. Clayborn, did you ever have a discussion about these grievances outside of a formal union meeting?"

"Yes, with Galen Small."

"Tell the jury what happened."

Again, Robert faced the jury. "One morning, I informed Mr. Small that the head librarian called in sick. I asked him if he would lock up that evening. He looked at me and said, 'Massa feelin' poorly this morning?' I told him he was not funny and to stop. He asked if he could. . . ."

Inez interrupted. "Your Honor, I must object to Mr. Pratt's examination of this witness."

Judge VanCulver's eyes widened. "Overruled."

"But, Your Honor. . . ."

Judge VanCulver interrupted and glared furiously at Inez. He yelled, "Ms. Connors, I have ruled, now sit down."

Inez sat down. *Fuck you. Go back to sleep, you fat bastard,* she thought.

Douglas' superior grin was maddening.

Beverly squinted at Douglas.

Douglas rubbed his hands together and instructed Robert to continue.

Robert exhaled. "Like I was saying, I told Mr. Small he wasn't funny. He asked if he could speak to me off the record. He asked if we could talk, brother-to-brother, black to black and I agreed." Robert cleared his throat and continued. "Mr. Small asked why was I trying to kiss up to the white man. He said when white people look at me they see the same thing when they look at him—a nigger."

Still seated in her chair, Inez hollered, "Objection, Your Honor. This is strictly hearsay."

Douglas turned toward the Judge. "Your Honor, a conversation between Mr. Clayborn and Mr. Small is not hearsay. Mr. Clayborn is telling what happened firsthand, not second."

"Overruled. Answer the question Mr. Clayborn." Judge VanCulver instructed.

Robert covered his mouth and coughed. "Would you please repeat the question."

A smile twitched the corners of Douglas' mouth. "What was your response to Galen Small when he said white people see a nigger when they look at you?"

"I said I don't see color, I see people. He said I was a sellout and that sleeping with a white woman is one thing, but to marry one is totally wrong." Robert exhaled. "Mr. Small told me I needed to go back to school and learn Black history."

"What did you say?"

"I looked at him, shook my head, and walked away."

"Do you know why Mr. Small dislikes you?'

"Yes."

"Tell us, please."

"When the job for head librarian became vacant, Mr. Small applied for the position. I gave the position to the most qualified applicant who happened to be white."

"Mr. Clayborn, let me shift your attention to Ella Walker. Did Mrs. Walker ever speak to you about Ms. Reinhart's treatment of Bryce Monday?"

"No."

"Did Mr. Small?"

"Never."

"Did Ms. Harris?"

"No, she did not."

"Did you ever see Ms. Reinhart inappropriately handle Bryce Monday or any other child?"

"I've never witnessed Jennifer Reinhart display any ill behavior toward Bryce Monday, or any of the children in her classroom."

"Have you ever had conversation with Beverly Monday about her son?"

"Yes."

"When and what were the circumstances?"

"It was back in January this year. I called Ms. Monday because Bryce was spitting on the bus and it had to stop. I told Ms. Monday that if it didn't I would consider suspension."

"And did you suspend Bryce?"

"No."

"Why not?"

"After talking to Ms. Reinhart, she convinced me that a suspension was not necessary because Bryce wouldn't understand. Ms. Reinhart explained to me that the spitting was probably an uncontrollable reaction due to Bryce's disability. I thought about what she said and decided to follow her advice."

Douglas examined the jury. "So it was Jennifer Reinhart who convinced you not to suspend Bryce Monday?"

Inez leaped to her feet. "Your Honor, may counselor and I please, approach the bench?"

"Very well."

Inez rushed up to the bench. "Your Honor, Mr. Pratt knows this has nothing to do with the charges. He's trying to undermine the jury by diverting their attention from the abuse. Please stop this line of questioning." Inez pleaded.

Douglas spoke calmly. "With all due respect, Your Honor, I think it's important that the jury know about the relationship between the defendants and the accusers."

"Both of you stop this wrangling," Judge VanCulver warned. "I'm going to allow you to continue Mr. Pratt, but do hurry. It's getting late and I would like to get home in time for supper."

Inez spun around on the ball of one foot and returned to her seat. Beverly leaned towards Inez, and whispered, "What's going on?"

Inez spoke softly in Beverly's ear. "Judge VanCulver agreed to let Mr. Prick, excuse me, I mean Mr. Pratt, continue with his line of questioning."

Douglas returned to the lectern. "So, Mr. Clayborn, it was Jennifer Reinhart who prevented you from suspending Bryce Monday?"

"Yes. After Ms. Reinhart explained Bryce's condition, I understood."

Beverly eyed him with tight lips and beady eyes, obviously upset at Mr. Clayborn's testimony.

Inez looked at Jennifer. Jennifer stared at Robert and nodded. Douglas had scored big time with the jury and Judge VanCulver.

Judge VanCulver had set a record, he'd not taken even forty winks today.

Douglas flipped through his notepad, before looking up at Judge VanCulver. "Your Honor, I have no further questions."

Judge VanCulver said, "Your witness, Ms. Connors."

Inez stood and approached the witness. "Mr. Clayborn, you told us Mrs. Walker never came to you to discuss Ms. Reinhart's abusive behavior towards Bryce Monday?"

"That's correct. She never did."

"Mr. Clayborn, isn't it true that Mrs. Walker pleaded with you to talk to Jennifer Reinhart and Beverly Monday?"

"No, she never came to me."

"You told Mrs. Walker to leave it alone. Bryce was going to a different school in fall and you already had grievances filed against you and you didn't want any more trouble." Inez raised her voice slightly. "Isn't that the truth?"

Calmly, Mr. Clayborn said, "No, I never said those things."

Douglas spoke from his seat. "Objection. The witness has already answered the question."

"Sustained."

Inez stared at Robert. She went back to the table, grabbed a notepad, then returned to the lectern. "Have you ever seen Ms. Reinhart abuse Bryce?"

Douglas stood. He interrupted before Robert could answer. "Your Honor, I must object again. My client has already answered that question in my direct examination and now Ms. Connors is asking the same question in cross."

Inez interrupted. "Your Honor, I withdraw the question."

Inez paced from one end of the witness box to the other end. "Mr. Clayborn, have you ever heard her yelling at Bryce?"

"No. Never."

"So it's your testimony that Ella Walker never spoke to you about Jennifer Reinhart?"

Still calm. "That's my testimony. She never did."

Inez exhaled.

As Inez turned to walk away, Robert blurted out, "Just because she calls the children retards doesn't mean she's a child abuser."

Inez halted. She'd gotten the break she'd hoped for. Inez whirled around. "What did you say?"

Douglas objected.

Judge VanCulver frowned. "To what, Mr. Pratt? Overruled. Continue, Ms. Connors."

Inez nodded. "Thank you. What did you say, Mr. Clayborn?"

Robert stared at Douglas.

Inez walked to within three feet of the witness stand. "Mr. Clayborn, I'll ask you again, what did you say just now?"

"Answer the question, Mr. Clayborn," Judge VanCulver ordered.

Robert still didn't respond. He nervously turned to the jury, who also appeared to be waiting for an answer.

Inez eyeballed Robert. "You said just because Ms. Reinhart calls the children retards doesn't mean she's a child abuser. Isn't that what you said?"

Robert still would not respond. Judge VanCulver had already overruled Pratt's objection, Robert had to answer the question.

Inez turned to the Judge. "Your Honor, please instruct the witness to answer the question."

"Mr. Clayborn, answer the question." Judge VanCulver directed.

Robert gazed at Susan, then Inez.

The courtroom was silent. Inez exhaled. "I'll ask you again. You said just because Ms. Reinhart calls the children retards doesn't mean she's a child abuser. Isn't that what you said?"

Softly, Robert answered, "Yes."

"Louder, Mr. Clayborn, so the jury can hear you."

"Yes."

"Mr. Clayborn, didn't Mrs. Walker tell you that Ms. Reinhart uses the word retard when she refers to the children in her classroom?"

"No, she didn't."

"Then how do you know?"

Robert removed his bifocals and wiped sweat from his face.

"Mrs. Walker said it the other day in court when she testified."

"Mr. Clayborn, Ella Walker never made that statement in court. Mrs. Walker said Ms. Reinhart calls the children names. She never used the word retard. I can have her testimony read by the court reporter. Mr. Clayborn, please," Inez looked at the jury with sympathy. "Don't waste the court's time. Just tell us how you know."

Robert stared at the floor and wouldn't respond.

"Mr. Clayborn, you know that Ms. Reinhart calls the children in her classroom retards because Mrs. Walker told you that when she spoke to you about Jennifer Reinhart's abusive behavior. Didn't she?"

Robert sighed and said, "Yes."

Booming murmurs in the courtroom prompted Judge VanCulver to bang his gavel, and yell, "Order in the Court."

When the courtroom became silent, Judge VanCulver instructed Inez to continue.

For the first time since the trial, Douglas appeared to be speechless.

Susan seemed puzzled by Robert's testimony.

"Mrs. Walker told you this when she spoke to you about Ms. Reinhart's behavior towards Bryce Monday. Mr. Clayborn, you told Mrs. Walker you weren't going to do anything and you threatened her, if she pursued it. Isn't that the truth, Sir?"

Robert crossed, then uncrossed his legs. "Yes." He said.

"Mr. Clayborn, why would you not investigate Ella Walker's complaint? Why didn't you tell Bryce's mother?"

Tears rolled down Beverly's cheeks.

"I talked to Ms. Reinhart and she assured me Mrs. Walker's allegations were false. That's why I didn't tell Ms. Monday. I didn't want any more trouble."

"Mr. Clayborn, why would you lie about talking to Mrs. Walker?"

Robert leaned forward and focused in on Inez. "Please leave me alone."

Douglas stood. "Your Honor, Ms. Connors is badgering the witness."

"Mr. Pratt, sit down and don't get up again." Judge VanCulver ordered. "Your objection is overruled." Judge looked at the witness. "Answer the question, Mr. Clayborn."

Mildly, Robert said, "I couldn't. I wanted to," he glanced at the jury, "but I just couldn't."

Inez watched Robert. "What stopped you? Or who stopped you?"

Robert stuttered. "I didn't think it would go this far."

"Mr. Clayborn, who stopped you from telling the truth?"

Inez glanced around the courtroom and Mora Abernathy sat on the edge of her seat.

Susan Clayborn stared at her husband. Inez realized that other than Susan, the only other person that had influence over Robert was his boss, Mora Abernathy. Inez turned around, her eyes fixated on Robert. "Was it Mora Abernathy, Mr. Clayborn?" Is she the one who stopped you from telling the truth?"

Susan frowned. She sat with one leg in the aisle as if ready to leap from her seat and rescue her husband from Inez.

Inez figured it had to be Mora because of Robert's hesitation. If it weren't, he would have quickly answered no.

"Mr. Clayborn, before you answer, please remember you're under oath. Was it Mora Abernathy that prevented you from telling the truth?"

Robert lowered his head.

There was piercing jabber in the courtroom. Judge VanCulver grabbed his gavel.

Mora sat back in her seat, crossed her legs at the knee, and frowned at Robert.

Susan appeared confused. She glanced at Mora, then Robert. Judge VanCulver banged his gavel and demanded silence in the court.

Inez approached Robert. "Mr. Clayborn, why would Ms. Abernathy tell you to keep quiet?"

Robert dropped his head, studied the floor.

"Is it because Ms. Abernathy never monitored Ms. Reinhart? If you admitted to your conversation with Ella Walker, and if Ms. Reinhart is convicted, the blame ultimately would lie with Ms. Abernathy because she hired Jennifer Reinhart. Is that why Mora Abernathy wanted you to lie?"

"Yes," Robert said softly.

"Did she threaten you?" Inez asked.

Robert sighed. "Yes."

"How?"

Robert peered up at the ceiling.

Judge VanCulver leaned toward Robert. "Answer the question, Mr. Clayborn. Tell the court how Ms. Abernathy threatened you."

Robert wiped sweat from his forehead. "She said she'd tell my wife."

Inez glanced at the jury, then at Robert. "Tell your wife what?"

Robert squirmed in his chair.

Inez surveyed the jurors. Ruth Beckom sighed heavily and rested her folded arms on her plump belly. John Williams twirled the end of his gray beard. Tianna Adams picked lint from her sweater. It was obvious the jurors were as tired of Robert Clayborn's procrastination as Inez.

Inez lifted her foot slightly out of her shoe. The high heels had taken a toll on her feet and she desperately wanted to sit down. It had become quite evident to her how Mora Abernathy blackmailed Robert Clayborn.

Inez's voice amplified. "Mr. Clayborn, did you have an affair? Is that what Ms. Abernathy threatened to tell your wife?"

Robert snatched his bifocals off his face and screamed. "Yes, damn you. Are you satisfied? I answered your question."

Again, the courtroom rang with chatter. Judge VanCulver banged his gavel several times before order returned. "I cleared this courtroom the other day and I'll do it again if this persists."

In the midst of the commotion, Inez arrived at another startling conclusion about Robert Clayborn. "Mr. Clayborn, how did Ms. Abernathy know you committed adultery?"

Douglas remained seated and yelled, "Objection. The witness has already admitted Ms. Abernathy's threat to expose his affair. There's no need to hear the details, Your Honor."

Inez didn't bother to offer an argument to Pratt's objection. She was confident of what Judge VanCulver's ruling would be.

"Overruled. Answer the question, Mr. Clayborn."

Douglas' perfect posture became slumped as he leaned forward in his seat. He waited with the rest of the courtroom for Robert's answer.

Robert stared at Susan. She gazed at him and not once attempted to clear her face of the gushing tears.

Inez glanced at Beverly whose eyes were fixed on Robert. She turned towards Robert again. "How did Mora Abernathy know about your affair?"

Robert's eyes filled with tears.

Gently, Inez said, "Mr. Clayborn, Ms. Abernathy knew about your affair because you had the affair with her. Didn't you?"

Judge VanCulver banged his gavel to warn the courtroom to keep quiet before they erupted.

Robert's head hung low. He covered his face with his hands and gasped for air as he started to weep. He cried, "Yes. God help me, yes."

Susan ran from the courtroom.

"No further questions, Your Honor."

"Redirect, Mr. Pratt?"

"No, Your Honor."

"You may step down, Mr. Clayborn," the Judge said.

Robert lifted his head and stood.

Judge VanCulver adjourned court until nine a.m. tomorrow.

CHAPTER TWENTY-NINE

Inez was thirty-five minutes late for her MADD meeting. Robert Clayborn's testimony had shocked everyone.

Today her MADD group would be passing out flyers explaining their cause and soliciting new members. When Inez arrived, the members were mingling amongst themselves, patiently waiting for her.

Inez walked to the front of the room and immediately received everyone's undivided attention. "I apologize for being so late. You know I've been in court all week with the child abuse case. The trial should be coming to an end soon."

Debra McCall asked, "How's it going?"

"Well, it's up and down. It's really hard to judge. Just say a prayer for the little boy who was hurt. I couldn't do anything to save my little girl, but I can sure as hell try to get this woman out of the school system so she doesn't hurt another child and make the system pay for hiring an incompetent."

"You have our support." Debra said.

The members clapped in agreement.

* * *

Beverly decided to go to Martin's. She wanted desperately to talk to him. She needed to make him understand and forgive her. She also knew Martin would be pleased with the outcome of the trial today.

She parked in front of Martin's house around nine o'clock p.m. All the lights were out. Beverly got out of the car and rang the doorbell several times and got no answer.

Beverly went back to her car and sat for about fifteen minutes and still no sign of Martin. Angry at his avoidance and refusal to discuss their situation, Beverly hit the steering wheel with her fist and drove off.

* * *

When Robert returned home that evening after his testimony, he found Susan packing.

"Baby, we have to talk," he pleaded.

Susan never responded. She flung her suitcases on their bed and emptied her drawers into the suitcases.

Robert grabbed Susan by the arm. "Talk to me, please."

Susan snatched herself away from him. "How could you, Robert? How could you betray me?" She started to cry but didn't stop packing.

Robert followed her around their bedroom. He put his hands on her shoulders and she jerked away again.

Susan yelled. "Don't you touch me. Don't ever touch me again. You disgust me."

Robert sat on his side of the bed with his head down and started to cry. "I love you, Susan. I'm sorry. I swear to God, it only happened once."

Susan stopped packing and looked at him. "You think because it happened once that makes it okay." She swallowed. "I wish I had never been in court today. I sat next to your lover." She screamed. "You admitted in court that you slept with the woman sitting next to your wife. You make me sick. The sight of you is repulsive."

Susan closed and locked her suitcases and sat them in front of their bedroom door. She walked over to her side of the bed and grabbed her purse. They looked at each other, both teary-eyed. Robert asked, "where's Eric?"

"I called my parents and told them what happened. Eric is with them, which is where I'm going now. They've met their grandson for the first time and look at the circumstances that caused it."

"Susan, I'll do anything, but please...."

Susan interrupted. "There's nothing for you to do. You've done enough. My parents were right about you. I chose you over my family. All I wanted from you was your love and you couldn't give that." She cried.

"Susan, I do love you." Robert stood and walked to the other side of the bed. "I'm begging you, please let me make it up to you."

Susan walked over to the door and picked up her suitcases. "It's too late. You can't ever make this up to me, or your son. Good-bye, Robert."

Robert started towards the door. He grabbed Susan's arm. "I won't let you leave me."

Susan yanked free. "You should've thought about that before you betrayed me." She began to cry again. "That poor little boy. I believe he was abused and I believe you and your lover knew it. If you have any decency left inside, you won't let that teacher or the school system get away with what happened to that child." Susan left.

Robert dropped to his knees and exploded into tears.

* * *

Inez's phone rang around three-thirty a.m. An anonymous caller shared shocking information with Inez. If true, this information could prove beneficial to the case. Inez immediately called Joey.

CHAPTER THIRTY

Inez decided the anonymous phone caller could not be used as a reliable source. The information may or may not be true. If it was, it would help Inez's case, but if it wasn't, she knew it could be damaging.

Beverly didn't look over her shoulder for Martin. Martin hadn't been in court since the day she testified and it was apparent he wouldn't be in court today.

Robert sat quietly with his hands in his lap. He watched Douglas flip through the pages of his notepad in preparation of his next witness.

Mora sat behind Douglas, legs crossed, arms folded.

Mr. Evans seated the jurors and Judge VanCulver instructed Douglas to call his next witness.

"I call Jennifer Reinhart to the stand." Jennifer stood at attention, glanced around the courtroom, then walked up to the stand to be sworn in. She wore a navy blue sailor dress.

Douglas walked up to the lectern. "State your full name for the record."

"Jennifer Rose Reinhart."

Inez thought, *What a beautiful name for such a mannish woman.*

Douglas proceeded. "What is your occupation?"

"I'm a teacher."

"Where were you last employed?"

"Carter Elementary School in the cognitive disabled classroom."

"Ms. Reinhart, how long have you been in the teaching profession?"

"Eight years."

"Describe for the jury a typical day in your classroom."

Jennifer cleared her throat and addressed the jury. "The focus is to develop life skills like grooming, bathing, dressing and toileting. We try to create a safe and predictable environment for the children."

Joey looked at Inez. They both knew Jennifer had been well rehearsed. She spoke like she was reading from a book.

Beverly rolled her eyes at Jennifer.

"Do you know Bryce Monday?" Douglas asked.

"Yes."

"How do you know him?"

"He was a student in my classroom at Carter Elementary School."

"How many students did you have in your classroom?"

"Five, including Bryce."

"Anyone else?"

"Yes, the HCA."

"What is an HCA?"

"HCA stands for Handicapped Children's Assistant."

"And who was the assistant in your classroom?"

"Ella Walker."

"Now, Ms. Reinhart, you know you're here because of the charges filed by Bryce's mother?"

"Yes."

"Do you know Bryce's mother, Beverly Monday?"

"Yes, I do."

"Did you call Ms. Monday on the last day of school to request a meeting?"

"No."

Beverly leaned over and whispered in Inez's ear. "She's lying, can't you do something." Inez gently patted Beverly on her hand, as if to say, "Don't worry, we'll have our turn."

"Ms. Reinhart, did you ever have conversation with Ella Walker regarding your treatment of Bryce Monday?"

"Yes."

"What happened?"

"Mrs. Walker didn't like taking instructions from me."

"Why not?"

"I guess because she's older, she doesn't feel comfortable with me being in charge."

Inez yelled from her seat. "Objection. Purely speculation. The witness's opinion is not a statement of fact. I would ask that Your Honor strike her last remark from the record."

Judge VanCulver peered at Candace and instructed her to strike Jennifer's last statement from the record. Judge VanCulver then looked at the jurors. "Jurors please disregard the last statement made by the witness. Continue Mr. Pratt."

Inez's lips tightened. She always hated when a jury was ordered to disregard a remark. Inez knew that would not change what was said and heard by all in the courtroom.

"Ms. Reinhart, Mrs. Walker said, you abused Bryce Monday."

"I've never abused any child."

Beverly gazed at Jennifer with squinted eyes.

"Did you ever grab Bryce Monday?"

"No."

"Did you ever shake him?"

"No."

"Did you ever squeeze his hand?"

"No."

"Did you ever put your knee in his back?"

"No."

"Does Bryce have behavior problems?"

"He's had tantrums."

"Beverly Monday testified that she visited the classroom frequently."

"Yes, she did."

"Did she make an appointment?"

"No. I told Ms. Monday that she could come visit any time. There was no need to make an appointment. Bryce is her child. She has that right."

"Out of all the unannounced visits, did Ms. Monday ever express disapproval?"

"Never."

"Did Ms. Monday ever say anything in regards to your instruction?"

"The only thing she'd ever said was that Bryce liked me and she was glad he had someone she felt comfortable with."

"Did Ms. Monday ever say anything else?"

"No. Nothing."

"No further questions. Your witness counselor." Douglas sat down.

Inez stood and walked to the lectern with a folder in her hand.

"Ms. Reinhart, what is your education?"

"I have a Bachelor's Degree in Education."

"Does that Bachelor's Degree cover education of the cognitively disabled children?"

"No."

"Do you have any additional training in this area?"

"Yes."

"What?"

"I'm presently in night school at Melbourne University working towards my Master's Degree."

"But, you don't have it now and you didn't have it when you were Bryce's teacher. Correct?"

"Yes."

Inez shook her head. "Were you qualified to teach in the cognitive disabled classroom at Carter Elementary School during the time Bryce Monday was a student?"

"Yes, I was."

"Ms. Reinhart, you don't have a Master's Degree. You admitted that you have not taken any additional training, but you still say you're qualified."

Douglas leaped to his feet. "Objection!"

"Sustained."

"Ms. Reinhart, how could you be qualified to teach severely handicapped children when you don't have the education or the training that is mandated by the State of Wisconsin? Tell the jury."

"I have...."

Inez interrupted, "Please look at the jury." Inez figured if Jennifer was going to lie, she would at least have her face the jury so they could see her face.

"I have hands on experience. I do have a teaching degree."

Inez was fed up with this liar. It was time for Jennifer's actions to speak louder than her words. Inez walked over to Joey and he handed her the life-size doll of Bryce.

"Since you insist you're qualified, please step down and take the doll."

Jennifer did as instructed.

"Show the courtroom how you would stop a child of Bryce's capacity from hurting himself during a tantrum."

Puzzled, Jennifer asked, "What?"

"How would you control a child like Bryce Monday if he was having a tantrum?"

"It's hard because this is a doll, not the real thing."

Beverly frowned. She bit down on her bottom lip in anger. Jennifer had told one lie after another.

"Try." Inez insisted.

Jennifer stared at the doll, then at the jury. She turned toward Douglas for help.

"Objection." Douglas stood. "Your Honor, my client has already explained that. . . ."

Judge VanCulver interrupted. "I know what your client explained. Overruled." Judge VanCulver looked at Jennifer. "Try, Ms. Reinhart."

Inez repeated. "Are you familiar with the techniques used to restrain children like Bryce?"

"No."

Inez took the doll. "Please take the stand."

Jennifer's face was red. It was evident Inez had irritated her.

Obviously upset, a wrinkle creased Beverly's brow.

Inez paged through her notes. "You don't know the techniques used to restrain children like Bryce Monday because you've never been trained how to use those techniques. Do you even know the names of them?"

Beverly began to breathe faster and glared at Jennifer.

Jennifer stared at Inez. "No, but that doesn't mean I abused him."

"Did Bryce's mother tell you that he didn't like milk in a cup?"

"Yes."

"How did you feel about that?"

"I didn't have a problem."

"Ms. Reinhart, you didn't have a problem with Bryce's mother, but you had a problem in the classroom, and that's why you and Mrs. Walker clashed."

"No. That's not true."

"Why did you call the children in your classroom retards?"

"I never did." Jennifer said sarcastically. "Ella Walker is a liar."

Inez quickly flipped through her notes. She had lost patience with this woman. She wasn't sure if Jennifer's testimony coupled with Robert Clayborn's and Mora Abernathy's was enough. Inez and Joey had decided that they would not use the information from the anonymous caller. If it weren't true, it could cost them the case. Inez couldn't risk it.

Jennifer crossed her arms and stared at Inez as if to say, "You might as well give up."

Inez sat down. "No further questions."

Judge VanCulver looked in Douglas' direction. "Redirect, Mr. Pratt?"

Douglas remained seated. "Just one question. Ms. Reinhart, you stated earlier that there were five children in your classroom at Carter Elementary."

"Yes. I have four now."

"Why are their less children in the cognitive disabled classrooms than the normal classrooms?"

"To give the children as much individualized attention as possible."

"No further questions."

Before Judge VanCulver could ask Inez if she wanted to re-cross examine Jennifer, Inez stood and walked to within a few inches of the witness stand and glared at Jennifer. "How long have you been a teacher at Pleasant Grove Elementary School?"

"I don't work at that school."

"Ms. Reinhart, Ms. Abernathy testified that you were suspended with pay pending the outcome of this trial. The truth is that you are still working in Melbourne Public School System at Pleasant Grove Elementary under Ms. Abernathy's supervision. Isn't that true? Before you answer Ms. Reinhart, I want to remind you that Ms. Abernathy has already perjured herself. You are still under oath."

Douglas sprang to his feet. "Your Honor, I. . . ."

Judge VanCulver interrupted, "Overruled. Answer the question, Ms. Reinhart. Are you teaching at Pleasant Grove?"

Jennifer showed no emotion. She was as calm as she was when she took the stand. She looked at Inez and calmly said, "Yes."

Inez pivoted towards the jury. Margaret Thatcher shook her head. Erica Dankmeyer removed her glasses and frowned.

Inez observed Beverly's clenched fists and teary eyes. She turned back to Jennifer. "Your Honor, I have no further questions of this woman."

Inez sat.

Judge VanCulver ordered Jennifer to step down.

Douglas rested his case.

Judge VanCulver announced that summations would begin tomorrow at nine a.m.

Beverly watched Jennifer with squinted eyes. The anger wrinkled her forehead and tightened her lips. Beverly thought about Bryce's first day at Carter Elementary School when she met Jennifer for the first time. She remembered how nice Jennifer appeared. Beverly imagined Bryce screaming in pain at the hands of this vile and evil woman. Beverly remembered the day she questioned Jennifer about Bryce's busted lip. She visualized Jennifer's knee in Bryce's back, causing it to bruise. All the lies and deceit made Beverly burn with anger.

As Jennifer stepped down from the witness stand, she shot a taunting smile at Beverly. That was the first time since the trial Jennifer had made any real eye contact with Beverly. Beverly remembered reading about the teacher that was found not guilty of abusing her student. She replayed in her mind the bruise on Bryce's back.

In the blink of an eye Beverly vaulted from her seat and found her hands locked around Jennifer's throat.

Beverly's one-hundred-thirty pounds forced Jennifer down to the floor. Beverly yelled, "I trusted you. How could you hurt my child? You bitch. I could kill you."

The people in the courtroom jumped to their feet, noise reached the level of a roar.

Beverly released Jennifer's throat. Jennifer coughed. Beverly rolled Jennifer over face down, pulled her arms behind her back and held them in place with her knees. Beverly pushed Jennifer's face to the floor and screamed, "How does it feel?"

Inez and Joey watched in shock.

Judge VanCulver banged his gavel repeatedly. He ordered Officers Edwards and Olson to restrain Beverly.

Beverly continued to cry. "I hate you. How does it feel to be in pain, Bitch."

CHAPTER THIRTY-ONE

Inez and Joey went back to the office to work on Inez's summation.

Joey asked Inez, "How could Beverly lose it like that?"

Inez sighed. "I don't know. Maybe she just couldn't take it anymore. To stay calm, look at Jennifer and know she's lying, I imagine was hard to do."

Joey nodded in agreement. "I think Beverly hurt the case with her outburst. She's lucky Judge VanCulver released her after the officers managed to calm her down."

"That's why I have to make up for her outburst in my summation."

"By the way, Inez, I thought you weren't going to use the information from the anonymous caller. I thought you didn't want to take a chance."

"I wasn't, but when Jennifer told Douglas that she had four children in her classroom, I figured it had to be true. I had to take a chance." How could she, if she's been suspended?"

There was a knock at the door.

Joey opened the door. It was Connie.

"Guys, I'm sorry to bother you, but there's someone here to see you."

"Who is it?" Joey asked.

Connie replied, "I was told to say it's the anonymous caller. I guess you know what that means?" She opened the door wider to expose a short, pale-skinned, dark brown-haired woman dressed in an olive green pants suit.

"Hello, Ms. Connors, I'm the anonymous caller. I'm the one who called and informed you Jennifer still worked for Melbourne Public School System."

Joey asked. "Why didn't you come forth with the information earlier?"

"Joey, wait." Inez warned. "Please come in, Miss."

"My name is Helene Dunbar. I'm the receptionist at the school board, or I used to be. I can't stay. I only wanted to make sure that Mora and the rest of them get what they deserve."

Inez shook her hand. "Thank you very much. But why didn't you let us know sooner?"

"I really didn't want to get involved. I thought the eye witnesses to the abuse of the little boy, and the fact that Jennifer Reinhart did not have proper training, would be enough to convict all of them. The other attorney kept finding ways to cover up their lies. I hate Mora Abernathy. She's a bitch and a home wrecker."

Joey asked. "You knew about her affair with Robert Clayborn?"

"No, I didn't know. I know she's a home wrecker because the tramp slept with my husband, too."

* * *

Beverly went to Sharon's house. She didn't want to be alone. She arrived at Sharon's around five-fifteen. Sharon, Tyler and Bryce had just finished dinner and were about to watch television when the doorbell rang.

When Sharon opened the door, Beverly fell in her sister's arms and burst into tears. "Oh Sharon, I think I blew the case."

"Come in Beverly and tell me what happened." Beverly and Sharon went into the living room and sat down.

Beverly wiped her tears. "Where's Bryce?"

"He's watching television with Tyler."

"I don't want Bryce to see me crying. Not that he'd understand, but I still don't want him to see me like this."

"So what happened today," Sharon asked.

"They're all done with testimony. Tomorrow will be summations, then the jury will decide. Sharon, I lost it again in the courtroom and attacked Jennifer."

Sharon's eyes widened. "You did what?" Why?"

"I don't know. In my mind, I saw that piece of shit abusing Bryce and before I knew it, my hands were around her fucking neck. I wanted to kill her. I really did. The next thing I remember is two police officers pulled me off her. She's still working in the school system. If she goes free, Sharon, I don't know what I'll do."

"She'll be convicted, but you have to stay focused and positive."

Beverly began to pace. "I can't believe this is happening. Did you know Carter used to be a church?"

"No, I didn't know."

Beverly plopped down on the couch. "The school had originally been St. James Catholic Church until about eleven years ago when Melbourne Public School System purchased the building and converted it to a school. Isn't that ironic? A place where people used to worship was actually converted into a hellhole where despicable and degrading acts of violence were inflicted on my child."

"Beverly, you must have faith. She'll pay for what she did to Bryce. You have to believe that Ms. Connors will get justice for Bryce. Have you heard from Martin?"

Beverly shook her head. "Not a word? It's like he vanished from the face of the earth."

CHAPTER THIRTY-TWO

It was sunny, but a cool and windy forty-five degrees. Weather predictions for the weekend indicated there would be no increase in the temperature.

Inez still wore her summer coat. She was determined to keep the heavy gear off for as long as possible. She arrived in court at eight-fifty a.m.

Douglas was already in court with his clients. He greeted Inez as she walked in. "Good morning, Ms. Connors."

Inez nodded, "Mr. Pratt."

Joey entered the courtroom and Beverly followed.

Inez read over her final plea to the jury until court reconvened at nine o'clock. Inez had instructed Beverly to have Sharon bring Bryce to court for her summation. The jurors needed to see Bryce again before they rendered a verdict.

Sharon and Tyler sat behind Beverly, and Bryce sat on Beverly's lap.

Judge VanCulver informed the jury that all testimony had been heard. He explained that each attorney would present a closing argument. Judge VanCulver explained to the jury that they would then be dismissed to discuss the case and decide on a verdict. He instructed Inez to proceed.

Inez stood, walked up to the jury box and greeted the jurors. Inez apologized for Beverly's outburst. She explained to the jury Beverly was distraught over what happened to her son. Any mother would be.

Inez explained Beverly never abused her son. Willie accused her of abuse, but the courts found no evidence and the case was dismissed. Inez further explained if Willie's story had been investigated, it never would have been mentioned in court. It was only a tactic used by Bryce's father after a failed attempt to blackmail Beverly for money.

She talked about how Douglas Pratt would have the court believe disgruntled employees concocted everything that happened to Bryce Monday in an effort to get revenge against the defendants.

Inez asked the jurors to question why would Robert Clayborn perjure himself, if abuse had not taken place? Why would Mora Abernathy lie about Jennifer Reinhart's continued employment in the Melbourne Public School System?

Inez pleaded with the jurors to remember Jennifer Reinhart had no idea what she meant when she asked her to demonstrate the different kinds of restraints used on cognitively disabled children who are out of control. Inez also reminded the jurors that Ms. Reinhart did not have proper education to teach cognitive disabled children, and the school system should be held accountable for their actions. Inez asked the jurors to recall the testimonies and demonstrations by Carter employees that, without a doubt, showed how this poor child screamed in agony due to Jennifer Reinhart's undue physical force.

Inez talked about how not only did the school system cover up the abuse to protect their reputation, it was also done to protect personal lives of those involved—the affair between Mora Abernathy and Robert Clayborn. Remember why Ms. Reinhart cancelled her meeting with Ms. Monday. There was no need to meet, since Mr. Clayborn told Mrs. Walker he was not going to do anything.

Inez stated, "Child abuse is the most despicable crime against a child, especially when that child is developmentally and cognitively disabled and cannot tell anyone what happened to him." She asked the jury not to forget Jennifer Reinhart first abused Bryce Monday in March. Beverly Monday returned to work from a leave of absence in February. During this leave, Ms. Monday made frequent unannounced visits. Inez pointed out that it was not a coincidence that abuse took place after Ms. Monday went back to work.

She told the jurors to remember that Jennifer Reinhart still works with children in the Melbourne Public School System. Inez told them Bryce Monday's disability prevented him from telling what was being done to him. Bryce couldn't say stop or leave me alone. He couldn't tell his mother. She asked the jury to be Bryce Monday's voice and put a stop to Jennifer Reinhart and the school system. The next child might not survive.

"Look beyond Jennifer's outward appearance." Inez said. "Her calm demeanor smothers the inner evil and abusive woman that she is. The element of her existence which allowed her to perpetrate the most despicable crime of all did come out in the classroom as she maliciously forced pain and suffering upon a helpless little boy."

Inez walked over to Bryce and stroked his curly hair then returned to the jury box. "Bryce Monday's civil rights were violated and I'm begging you to grant justice for this little boy by finding the defendants guilty."

Inez thanked the jury for their time and sat down.

Douglas rose and approached the jurors. "No abuse occurred." He asked the jury to remember one important thing, "If Jennifer Reinhart did all these horrible things to Bryce Monday, why didn't anyone call the police?" Douglas asked the jury to remember that it took months for these teachers to come forward.

Douglas mentioned that Beverly's attack on Ms. Reinhart was proof that these tendencies existed in her and she had a violent nature. He reminded the jury of Galen Small and his hatred of white people. "Mr. Small hated Robert Clayborn because he married a white woman, and because he was denied a position that was given to a white employee. This man would do anything to get revenge, even lie."

He asked the jury to think about one very important issue, "If Jennifer Reinhart really did abuse Bryce Monday, why didn't Ella Walker tell Bryce's mother? Mrs. Walker waited weeks instead of acting immediately to what she claims was abuse."

Inez looked at the jurors and interpreted they were giving thought to what Douglas had said.

Lastly, Douglas asked the jury to consider that each one of the witnesses, Ella Walker, Galen Small, and Agnes Harris had a conflict with either Jennifer Reinhart or Robert Clayborn and they used Bryce Monday as a way of getting revenge.

He asked the jury to render a verdict of not guilty and sat down.

Judge VanCulver turned to the jury. "Ladies and gentlemen of the jury, this phase of the trial has ended. You've heard testimony from several individuals regarding this case. Attorney Inez Connors and Attorney Douglas Pratt presented their summations. Now, ladies and gentlemen, from the evidence and testimony presented in this case, you will render a verdict."

The jurors were escorted out of the courtroom and Judge VanCulver banged his gavel and adjourned court.

* * *

The jurors took a vote by a show of hands before any discussion began to see where everybody's thoughts were. If it were unanimous they could go back into the courtroom, announce the verdict and go home to their loved ones they had not seen since the trial started a week ago.

Four of the twelve jurors, Denise Thatcher, Margaret Lewis, Ruth Beckom and Laurel Valentine voted "not guilty." Five of the jurors, Erica Dankmeyer, Dominic Santiago, John Williams, Annie Mae Wallace and Louis DeChambre, voted "guilty." The remaining three jurors, Maxwell Cane, Brenda Booker and Tianna Adams were undecided. One thing was certain, the jurors would not be going home today.

CHAPTER THIRTY-THREE

The trial had finally ended. After a week of listening to testimony and wiping her tears, Beverly was exhausted. The running back and forth to court, listening to witnesses testify about Bryce's abuse was finally over. Beverly was going to finally know if Jennifer Reinhart would be punished for her crime.

Beverly gave Bryce his bath and put him to bed around eight-thirty. Beverly kneeled down and kissed him. "I'm sorry, baby," she whispered. "Please forgive mommy for not protecting you." Beverly started to cry softly. "I swear I didn't know."

Bryce was asleep. Beverly took his hand. "You are the most important thing in my life. I love you more than life." She stroked Bryce's hair. "Bryce, you are so special and a blessing from God. Forgive me son. Please forgive me. I'll never let another soul hurt you again."

Beverly continued to stroke Bryce's hair. "Maybe it's good you don't know what's going on. I love you, my precious."

She wiped her tears and kissed Bryce on the forehead, then on his cheek. Bryce was still asleep. Beverly closed the door and left.

She went to the living room and was about to turn on the television when the doorbell rang. It was Sharon.

"Hi, what a nice surprise." Beverly said.

Sharon gave Beverly a hug and entered. "You were on my mind, so I wanted to see you."

"Sharon, you always know, don't you?" Beverly said.

"Know what?" Sharon asked.

They both sat on the couch.

Beverly smiled. "You always know when something's bothering me."

"Yeah, I do. Soon, it'll all be over and done with."

"Yeah." Beverly slid closer to Sharon.

"Oh, Sharon, I'm to blame for this."

"What do you mean?"

Beverly jumped up and screamed, "It's my fault. It's all my fault that she hurt Bryce."

Sharon sat with her head down and started to cry. "If it's your fault, Beverly, then it's my fault, too."

"Why?" Beverly asked.

"Just like you should've known, I should've known, too."

Beverly went over to the couch and sat beside Sharon. "I'm his mother."

"And I'm his aunt and his godmother. I couldn't love Bryce anymore if I had given birth to him. Don't you see, Beverly?" Sharon grabbed Beverly's hands. "I was the first person to see Bryce when he left school every day. I should've seen a sadness or something that told me he was in trouble. I should've sensed it."

Beverly snatched her hands from her sister's. "Sharon, don't."

"Don't what? Beverly, don't you understand the role of a godmother is to fill in and protect the child in the parent's absence? If anybody should've known, it was me." Her voice raised on the last words. "Isn't there a part of you that blame me?"

Beverly jumped up. "I won't listen to you talk like this. I don't want to hear it." She covered her ears. "Stop it Sharon. I mean it."

Sharon buried her face in her hands and began to cry.

Beverly raced back to the couch. She grabbed Sharon's forearms and started to shake her. "Stop it. I won't have you blaming yourself." Beverly began to cry too. "Sharon, I look at his little face and I wonder if he feels like I let him down. I wonder if he thinks why didn't I help him? Day after day, week after week, I sent Bryce to that school to be tortured. What kind of mother am I?" Beverly moaned. "I saw a bruise on his back and didn't do a damn thing."

Sharon held her sister tighter. Stroking Beverly's hair, Sharon began to rock Beverly like a baby. "We're both blaming ourselves for what happened to Bryce. The reality of it is it's no one's fault but Jennifer Reinhart."

Beverly continued to cry. "She told me he fell and busted his lip and I believed her." Beverly sank deeper in Sharon's arms, "Oh God, Sharon, I want to kill that bitch."

CHAPTER THIRTY-FOUR

When the phone rang at ten-twenty p.m., Inez knew it had to be either her parents or news that the jury had reached a verdict.

"Inez, Honey, how are you? Did I wake you?"

"I'm fine, Mom. I was sitting here thinking about the case. I was about to go to bed. How are you and Dad?"

"We're fine. Dad's asleep. How's it going, Honey? We haven't heard from you in a while."

"The case went to the jury yesterday." Inez sighed. "Now, I have to wait and see what happens."

"Do you think you'll win?"

"I honestly don't know, Mom. It was up and down throughout the whole trial. It could go either way."

"Dad and I will pray it goes your way."

Inez whimpered. "What she did to Bryce is unspeakable."

"Inez, dear, don't take it personally."

"I can't help it, Mom. I couldn't save my precious Allie the night she was killed by a drunk driver. And, now, maybe, I've failed this little boy, too."

"Win or lose, you didn't fail him. You told the court, the world, what his teacher did to him. You were his voice. And if the jury does find his teacher not guilty, I'm sure she'll think twice before harming another child. Just know that you did your best."

"Thanks, Mom."

"I wanted to check on you. I'll let you get some rest. Let us know what happens."

"I will. I love you Mom, and give Dad my love."

* * *

Inez didn't exercise in the morning. It was the first time in years she missed her five a.m. ritual. She overslept. She didn't realize how worn out she was from the stress of the trial. She didn't get up until seven o'clock. She showered and changed into her black satin pajamas. Inez sat in the living room with a cup of coffee when the doorbell rang. It was Joey.

He smiled. "I thought we could wait together."

"Come in, you always know when I need a friend." They hugged. He stepped inside and they sat on the couch.

"Want some coffee? Or how about breakfast?" she asked.

"Nothing for me."

Inez sipped from her cup. "What if we lose? Jennifer Reinhart will continue to work with children. She's already teaching at another school."

"Ella Walker waited so long before she reported Jennifer. The jury probably feels like she wouldn't have waited if Bryce was really being abused. I don't give a damn about proper procedure. If a child is being hurt, you do what you have to do to save him," Inez said. "You don't fucking wait weeks to do something."

Joey ran his fingers through Inez's hair. "Hey, calm down. Losing one battle is not losing the war. You can't give up."

Inez stroked Joey's cheek. "You always know what to say to make me feel better. Thank you, Joey."

Joey beamed. "It comes natural when I'm with you."

"I remember the day I came to see you after visiting Allie's grave. You were so caring."

Joey held Inez's face in his hands. "That's what friends are for and, besides, I care about you deeply."

They eyed each other and as Joey moved his lips closer to hers, he was interrupted by the phone. The jury had reached a verdict and court would resume tomorrow at nine o'clock.

CHAPTER THIRTY-FIVE

Inez was nervous. After a day and a half of deliberations, the jury had made a decision.

Inez sat in the courtroom and rubbed her hands together.

Douglas Pratt entered the courtroom and extended his hand to Inez. "Good luck, Counselor."

Douglas' clammy palms let Inez know that he, too, was nervous.

Beverly sat quietly and, from time to time, glanced over her shoulder for Martin. She was sure Martin knew the verdict was in and would be in court to hear it.

Sharon and Tyler arrived with Bryce. If the jury found Jennifer Reinhart and the school system not guilty, Sharon knew Beverly would need her support. Sharon and Tyler sat with Bryce in the third row behind Beverly.

Ella Walker, Agnes Harris and Jeffrey Garrison were all in court to hear the verdict.

When Judge VanCulver instructed Mr. Evans to escort the jury in, Joey leaned closer to Inez and whispered, "Remember, no matter what, you did your best. You told Bryce's story." Beverly nodded in agreement.

The door of the courtroom opened and all heads turned in that direction. Members of Inez's MADD group had arrived to hear the verdict. Debra McCall gave Inez a thumb's up as she and the others took seats in the back of the courtroom.

Inez breathed deeply and glanced at Robert Clayborn, Jennifer Reinhart and Mora Abernathy.

Robert sat with his head down, eyes fixated on the floor. Inez figured he must have been saying a prayer.

Jennifer picked at her fingernails, seemingly unconcerned about what was about to happen.

Mora sat in her usual position. She sighed, from time to time, as if she just wanted it to be over and done with.

Inez refused to look at the jurors as they entered the courtroom. If the verdict was not guilty, she was sure she'd see it on their faces.

Inez noticed a slight grin on Douglas Pratt's face as he watched the jurors enter. She wasn't sure what that meant. Maybe Douglas could see not guilty written all over the jurors' faces. Maybe Douglas smiled because he knew she watched him.

After the jurors were seated in the jury box, Judge VanCulver asked, "Ladies and gentlemen of the jury, it is my understanding that you have reached a verdict in this case. Is that correct?"

The foreman, Louis DeChambre, answered loudly, "That is correct, Your Honor."

"Mr. Foreman, please give the verdict to Mr. Evans." Judge VanCulver instructed.

Mr. DeChambre stood and handed a folded piece of paper to Mr. Evans. Inez glared at Mr. Evans as he delivered the paper to Judge VanCulver. She still refused to look at the jurors.

Judge VanCulver unfolded the paper, scanned it quickly, refolded the paper and handed it back to Mr. Evans. Will the defendants please rise."

Robert Clayborn wiped his forehead as he stood. Jennifer Reinhart rose to her feet, both arms at her side. Mora Abernathy lifted her body slowly.

"Mr. Evans, please read the verdict," Judge VanCulver directed.

Inez held Beverly's shaking hand.

Ella Walker stared at Jennifer Reinhart.

Agnes bowed her head, Bible in her lap as if to pray.

Sharon held Bryce's face to her bosom and stroked his hair.

Mr. Evans faced Jennifer Reinhart, Robert Clayborn and Mora Abernathy and proceeded to read the verdict. "We the jury, in the above mentioned case, find Jennifer Reinhart, Robert

Clayborn, Melbourne Public School System and Boelter Insurance Company guilty."

There was an uproar of approval in the courtroom. Inez hugged Beverly. Sharon dashed to her sister with Bryce in her arms and hugged her.

Beverly took Bryce and hugged him. Tyler wrapped his arms around Sharon, Beverly and Bryce.

Inez smiled at Joey.

Joey nodded. "I knew you'd win."

Tears flowed down Ella Walker's face.

Agnes hugged her Bible and cried, "Thank you, Master."

Douglas turned towards Robert Clayborn whose face was buried in his hands. Jennifer watched Robert and showed no emotion to the verdict. Mora shook her head in disbelief.

Judge VanCulver repeatedly banged his gavel to gain order. "Everyone be seated, immediately."

Judge began to speak to the defendants. "Jennifer Reinhart, you have been found guilty of child abuse."

Jennifer showed no remorse.

Judge VanCulver continued. "A violent act against a child is the worse possible crime. This conviction bars you from receiving a license or permit to operate as a child educator. It also, prevents you from obtaining employment, or continuing employment in a facility where access to children is part of the job duties.

Judge VanCulver cleared his throat. "In addition, Ms. Reinhart, I'm going to sentence you to the maximum of five years in prison, to be served at the Melbourne County Correctional Institution for Women. What you did to this child is unspeakable and the fact that Bryce Monday is cognitively disabled makes you less than a human being."

Judge VanCulver focused intensely at Robert Clayborn. "Mr. Clayborn, the fact that you knew makes you just as guilty as Ms. Reinhart."

Judge switched his attention to Mora Abernathy. "Ms. Abernathy, you hired a woman you knew was not qualified. You had no concern for the children in the classroom and you did everything that you could to cover it up. You, along with Mr. Clayborn, perjured yourselves to cover up this crime. Those charges will be dealt with at a later time."

Inez smiled.

Judge squinted at Jennifer, Douglas and Mora. "All of you were so busy trying to cover up and protect yourselves, you forgot about this child." He glanced at Bryce.

Bryce stared into space. Beverly wiped her tears.

Judge removed his glasses. "Melbourne Public School System's motto, Haven of Safety and Learning, is a joke."

Ella nodded in agreement.

Judge VanCulver continued. "Now comes the issue of damages. Bryce Monday suffered for weeks and endured tremendous pain. This child could not tell what was being done to him and that angers me immensely."

Judge VanCulver turned towards Beverly. "Ms. Monday, you placed your child in what you thought was an environment of safety. You had no way of knowing what he was going through."

Beverly started to cry.

Judge folded his arms. "There is no amount of money that could make up for the torture, pain and suffering your son endured. The Melbourne Public School System by way of Boelter Insurance Company is, hereby, ordered to pay the sum of one million dollars for each reported act of violence against this child, totaling three million dollars.

I'm also, awarding an additional five million dollars in punitive damages for Melbourne Public School System's actions in this case, for a total of eight million dollars."

Judge VanCulver ordered Officers Edwards and Olson to take Jennifer Reinhart into custody. He banged his gavel. "This court is adjourned."

CHAPTER THIRTY-SIX

It had been days since the trial ended and there was still no word from Martin. Beverly called Inez every day and he still had not been to the office. She left numerous messages at Martin's home.

She'd begun to accept the fact that Martin would never forgive her for not telling him he had a son. Martin was out of her life again, and this time for good.

Beverly sat at the kitchen table feeding Bryce chicken and potatoes. "I messed up, Bryce," she said. "I should've told Martin he was your dad."

Bryce stared at Beverly. "I know you don't understand, Sweetie." She fed him another spoonful of potatoes. "Well, Kiddo, it's just you and me again."

The doorbell rang. Beverly's first thought was Martin, but she knew it couldn't be. She opened the door, to Willie. She tried to close it, but he shoved the door open and knocked Beverly back a few feet. She stumbled but captured her balance before she fell to the floor.

Willie reeked of alcohol. His clothes were disheveled and dirty. His eyes were bloodshot.

Beverly yelled, "Get out, Willie."

Willie staggered in and left the door wide open. "I heard you won."

"No thanks to you. How could you tell them I abused my son?"

Willie walked towards Beverly. "Shut up, bitch." He growled. "How much did you get?"

Beverly backed up. "None of your damn business. How much did the school system pay you for the information you gave Attorney Pratt about me? Huh?"

Willie grabbed Beverly by her arms and shook her. "I said, how much did you get?"

Willie's harsh, stale breath stung Beverly's face. Bryce walked into the living room and Beverly pulled away from Willie. "You probably scared him with your loud voice. Why don't you just get out. You're drunk." She ran to Bryce and put her arms around him.

Willie staggered over towards Beverly and Bryce. "Let me see my son."

"No. You've been drinking. I don't want you around him when you're like this. In fact, I don't ever want you around him again." Beverly yelled, "Get out before I call the police."

Willie grabbed Bryce's hand. Bryce started to scream.

"Willie, let go of my son." Beverly pulled Bryce's hand from Willie's and headed for the opened door.

Willie moved between Beverly and the door. "You're not going anywhere."

"Please leave us alone. You're scaring my son."

Willie hollered, "He's my son, too."

At that moment, a voice boomed out, "No, he's my son." Martin stood in the doorway.

Willie turned towards Beverly. "Who's this mother fucker?"

Martin stepped inside and answered. "The one who's going to kick your ass if you ever bother Beverly or my boy again."

Beverly stared at Willie. "Bryce is not your son. I was pregnant when I met you. Get out of my house."

Willie looked at Martin, then at Bryce. "I never thought the retard was mine anyway." He staggered past Martin and rolled his eyes.

Martin spun Willie around, grabbed him by his collar and pushed him against the wall. Martin yelled. "The only retard I see in this room is you. Don't ever come back, because if you do, I'll be the one answering the door. I promise, you won't like the greeting." Martin yanked Willie from the wall, pushed him to the door and yelled, "Get out."

Willie slammed the door.

Martin rushed over to Bryce, picked him up and hugged him. He sat Bryce on the couch and kissed him on the forehead.

Nervous, Beverly stood with her arms folded as she watched Martin. Martin stared at her. A tear rolled down his cheek. Beverly started to cry.

Martin walked over to Beverly and wrapped his arms around her and whispered in her ear. "I love you."

CHAPTER THIRTY-SEVEN

Inez received numerous phone calls and letters regarding the outcome of the trial. She and Joey sat in her office and tackled the stack of mail that covered the top of her desk.

"Inez, are you going to read all this mail?" Joey asked.

"Yes, every single letter."

Joey folded his arms, shook his head. "You did good, Inez. I'm proud of you."

"I couldn't have done it without you, Joey. But you know, I've been thinking about how many other teachers of cognitively disabled children are not qualified to teach. I wonder how many of them have actually had the additional training required by the State of Wisconsin?"

"It sounds like you're up to something. What's on your mind?" Joey asked.

Inez began to pace. "Every time you've gone to a doctor's office, what's the one thing you always see on the wall?"

Joey thought for a few seconds. "I'm sorry, I don't know. I give up. What?"

"Don't you always see their credentials hanging on the wall? I used to think they were bragging, but, since this trial, I don't see it that way anymore. It's a comfort to know my doctor has had the training necessary to medically treat me correctly."

"Yeah, you're right. So what are you getting at?"

Inez stopped pacing and sat on top of her desk. "I'm saying these teachers should be required to display their credentials. It's just as important that you know the person hired to teach your child has had proper training, as it is with a doctor."

She stood again. "Even when I go to the beauty parlor, my beautician has her certificate on the wall. Why shouldn't teachers? Kids are graduating and can't read or even fill out an application for employment. I would love to see the credentials of their educators. I mean, how many more Mora Abernathys do we have out there who are knowingly hiring unqualified teachers?"

"That sounds like an issue worth pursuing." Joey said.

"I might just do that, Joey."

"I'll be right there by your side."

A knock came at the door. Connie opened it enough to poke her head through. "There's some people here that I know you both want to see."

Inez sighed and plopped down in the chair. "Connie, please, no more reporters. Send them away. Tell them to come back tomorrow."

Connie opened the door wider and Martin entered holding Bryce with Beverly at his side.

Inez jumped up. Smiling, she walked over and took Bryce from Martin's arms. Inez hugged Bryce, and smiled at Beverly and Martin. "It's good to see you two together again."

Joey shook Martin's hand and hugged Beverly. "I'm glad you straightened out your differences."

Beverly walked over to Inez. "I wasn't totally honest with you about Willie and I apologize for that."

"There's no need to talk about that. You won. It's over."

Beverly hugged Inez. "Thank you for everything."

Inez stared at Bryce, and for a moment, thought about her daughter. She smiled at Beverly. "Just be happy. Bryce is so lucky to have a mother and a father like you and Martin." Inez stood Bryce on the floor. Bryce tottered over to Martin.

Beverly's eyebrows shot upward. "Inez, you know?"

Inez pointed. "Look at the two of them. Bryce is the spitting image of Martin. How could I not know?"

Joey, Martin and Bryce joined Beverly and Inez. Beverly shook Joey's hand. "Thanks, and I need your help again."

Joey smiled. "Name it."

"Martin and I were talking and we'd like to use the majority of the money to set up scholarships to pay for training teachers for children like Bryce. Maybe, if there's money to pay teachers' education, something like this won't happen again."

Martin put an arm around Beverly. "We thought about setting up scholarships in my son's name."

Inez stroked Bryce's hair. "That's wonderful."

Beverly and Martin started towards the door. "We have to go now." Beverly said. "We just wanted to thank you two again."

Martin turned around. "I want the two of you in the front row of the church at our wedding. Understood?"

Inez giggled. "Understood."

Joey saluted. "Yes, Sir."

Beverly and Martin left.

Inez grinned at Joey. "We make a good team. Don't we?"

"Yes, we do."

Joey walked closer to Inez and extended his hand to her. "Before Martin and Beverly arrived, you were talking about pursuing issues. I have an issue to pursue with you."

Inez took Joey's hand. "And, what might that be?"

"The issue of you and me. We were interrupted the other night when we found out the jury had reached a verdict."

Joey wrapped his arms around Inez's waist. Inez smiled and stroked his cheek with the back of her hand. Their lips connected, this time, without interruption.

THE END

9 780738 816302

90000

ST. ALBERT PUBLIC LIBRARY
5 ST. ANNE STREET
ST. ALBERT, ALBERTA T8N 3Z9